MATT SPROUTS

AND

THE CURSE OF THE TEN BROKEN TOES

MATT SPROUTS

AND

THE CURSE OF THE TEN BROKEN TOES

MATT EICHELDINGER

Andrews McMeel
PUBLISHING®

Andrews McMeel Publishing
a division of Andrews McMeel Universal
1130 Walnut Street, Kansas City, Missouri 64106

www.andrewsmcmeel.com

24 25 26 27 28 LAK 10 9 8 7 6 5 4 3 2

Paperback ISBN: 978-1-5248-8869-5
Hardback ISBN: 978-1-5248-8870-1
Library of Congress Control Number: 2023943121

Editor: Erinn Pascal
Designer: Tiffany Meairs
Production Editor: Margaret Utz and Julie Railsback
Production Manager: Jeff Preuss
Special thanks to Wise Ink Creative Publishing and Sheila Smallwood

Made by:
Lake Book Manufacturing, LLC.
2085 North Cornell Avenue
Melrose Park, Illinois 60160, United States of America
1st Printing – 02/26/2024

ATTENTION: SCHOOLS AND BUSINESSES
Andrews McMeel books are available at quantity discounts with bulk
purchase for educational, business, or sales promotional use. For
information, please e-mail the Andrews McMeel Publishing
Special Sales Department: sales@amuniversal.com.

For Briana, Avery, and Evelyn
and our future adventures together.

LEMONS

My dad always says that when life gives you lemons, you're supposed to make lemonade. But what about when life gives you ten broken toes—then what do you do? Have an answer?

I didn't think so.

If you'd told me that one year I'd be using my toes to keep track of how many bad things happened to me, I would have laughed in your face. No, I would have pointed and laughed at your face. Or maybe I would've just ignored you because I thought you were confused or something.

It came true, though, the toe thing. It all came true. The Curse took more from me in one school year than anyone could have thought. My little brother blames me for what happened, but there is only one logical force to blame: the Curse.

Consider yourself lucky. I am going to tell you my story, and if you take notes, you might be able to avoid the misfortune I suffered last year. Seriously. Take out your notepad, sharpen a pencil. Get ready to learn.

I suppose, though, before I go any further, I should introduce myself.

My name is Matt Sprouts, and I'm the Cursed Kid.

CHAPTER 1
KARATE MOVES

Montrose, Colorado—that's where I'm from. If you are driving past it and blink, you might miss it. It sits in a valley surrounded by the San Juan Mountains, so everywhere you look you see a snowcapped ridge or peak. My house has the best view too. It's in a neighborhood just outside of town that sits on a hill above the Uncompahgre River. Tall aspen trees grow faster than the grass out there, and sometimes I forget I live next to anyone. It's a perfect place to grow up, and I wouldn't trade it for anything. Well, maybe ten fewer broken toes.

This is where the story begins, during the summer before sixth grade. June 1, to be exact, the day after my eleventh birthday. I set my alarm for 7:45 a.m. It gave me just enough time to pour a bowl of peanut butter cluster cereal and snuggle into our flower-covered green couch. This was my alone time. My time to watch and study ninjas during morning cartoons and brush up on my martial arts skills.

I love ninjas. Wait, is there a better word than love? Whatever it is, that's how I feel about ninjas. I can tell you all the facts too, like how they were amazing warfare experts in ancient Japan or how many weapons they knew how to use. I begged my parents to let me train to become a ninja, but the closest we could get was karate classes, which didn't last long. The instructor left town, which meant I could only watch TV and practice what I saw from cartoons.

Of course, I never practiced my moves on anyone. Once, I tried to karate chop Elliott, my soon-to-be third-grade brother, when he reached for some of my chips during a picnic, but Dad caught me.

"Take **THAT!** And **THAT!**" I yelled and flung my hand straight toward Elliott's face.

Before I could even get one hit, Dad grabbed the back of my shirt and yanked me to the ground.

"If you even think about doing that again, Saturday morning cartoons are done. Are we clear?" His finger was so close to my nose that I could smell the oil and dirt from his shop.

Dad seemed mad that day, but I knew exactly what he was trying to say. My karate moves were clearly too powerful to use on a person. So I decided to keep them to myself— most of the time.

Anyways, back to morning cartoons.

I turned to channel 9 and sat at the edge of the cushions, shoving spoonful after spoonful of peanut-buttery goodness

His eyes were barely open. "Mmmm, okay," he grumbled. Despite his lack of energy, he put on his shoes and followed me out the door. No kid could resist an invitation to play outside, even at 8:00 in the morning.

Eric is part of the Monkling family, who lives next door. He is a grade older than me and shares my love for karate, ninjas, and soccer. He's not as skilled as I am (I'm practically an expert at everything), but we have a good time together, and he's my best friend.

Eric and I *were* going to build a mud house in the creek out back, but we were interrupted by an unstoppable force.

"Hey, guys! What are you doing?" Jenna asked us from over the fence.

Ugh. Jenna, Eric's younger sister. She is a royal pain in the butt. She is a grade below me but acts like we are best friends and trails me everywhere.

"I said, 'What are you doing?'" she repeated.

"None of your business," Eric and I said together.

Jenna ignored our obvious get-lost hint. "Let's play tag!"

"C'mon, Jenna, you always say that. Go play tag with yourself," I insisted and threw some mud in her direction.

"But I want to play NOW!" she screamed. She shook the fence like a toddler in a playpen and began her usual assault of tears and screams.

It took a full hour of screaming, but she finally got her way. Since we didn't want to be the only ones suffering, we forced my brother, Elliott, and Eric's younger brother, Kyle, to play tag too.

"We can do whatever we want!" Kyle yelled. "You can't make me play with you!"

"Sure I can," Eric said and pinned Kyle down to the ground. "Here comes a big wet one!" Eric dunked his finger into his mouth and aimed it for Kyle's ear.

"Okay, okay, okay! We'll play!" Kyle pleaded. He never really stood a chance against Eric. Kyle was tiny for a third grader and spent most of his time drawing. He was pretty good at it too! Unfortunately for Kyle, drawing all the time didn't help build enough muscle to out-wrestle his brother. Besides drawing, Kyle usually hung out with Elliott, who stuck by his side no matter what.

"I'll play too," Elliott joined. It was a smart move. He knew a wet willy could have been in his future.

We all walked to the backyard, and the game started like we all knew it would.

Jenna was "it" and started chasing me. She only chased me. My mom said it was because she had a crush on me, but that didn't make any sense. Sometimes when we played, Jenna would chase me for up to an hour around our neighborhood while the rest of the kids found something else to do. And for that reason, tag was horrible.

I easily dodged her first swipe and sprinted to the back of the house. I darted around the brick corner and hid behind a row of prickly red bushes that lined the wall, making sure no one else saw where I went. I figured I could stay there and rest maybe a minute or two before Jenna spotted me. She was slower than syrup.

"Matt! Hey! Where are you? You can't hide—that's not fair!" a voice cried.

I peeked around the bush, and sure enough, it was Jenna. Only a few minutes into the game, and she was already crying. *What a baby*! I snickered at the thought.

"There you are!" Jenna confidently said, and through the thorns I could see her skipping toward me.

I must have made too much noise and given away my location. No time to dawdle. There was no way I was going to let Jenna touch me and make this game worse than it already was. I pushed off with both feet in the dirt and hurdled over the bush, but as soon as I hit the grass, my legs tangled. I stumbled awkwardly for a minute, then fell over.

I didn't have time to see what I tripped on. Jenna was within striking distance now: a decision had to be made. My heart thumped like a drum. The last thing I wanted was to get touched by her.

"Haha! I got you now!" Jenna giggled as she reached down to tag my shoulder.

Then it happened. My instincts suddenly took over. My body became numb, and I could feel each hair on my body stand straight up, like when you get goose bumps. Only this was more intense. Images of cartoon fighting moves flashed through my brain like a movie reel. **FLASH!** A high kick. **FLASH!** A low karate punch. **FLASH!** Backflip into a backhand punch. **FLASH!**

Adrenaline coursing through my veins, I stuck my leg out with lightning speed, dug my hands into the grass, and spun around so quick I got dizzy. In one swift motion, my ankle collided with the back of Jenna's, and I kicked both her feet out from under her. It was identical to a Saturday morning cartoon.

Jenna fell shoulder-first into the ground and lay motionless with her back toward the sun.

For a minute, I thought she might be dead.

Then, without warning, Jenna unleashed a massive scream, one that forced me to cover both my ears. It was like standing next to a fire alarm! I scuttled backward while my eyes vibrated back and forth and the hair on my neck stood up. The sound pierced the sky and traveled through the neighborhood. Although I could never prove it later, I think the sound shattered the white piggy bank in my bedroom.

"What's that sound?! It's making my ears bleed!" Eric yelled, trying to get his bearings.

Eric, Kyle, and Elliott appeared from behind the corner of the bushes with their ears covered.

"Jenna! What's wrong?" Eric begged as he tried to break the barrier of her screaming.

"Mmmm! Mmmmm!" was all Jenna could get out. Her face was stuck in the dirt.

Eric flipped her over so we could see, and his face immediately turned white. The collar of Jenna's pink daisy shirt was torn, and next to it was an oddly shaped bump on the top of her right shoulder. It formed a small mountain peak, like something was trying to pop out from beneath her skin.

One of Jenna's pigtails flopped into her mouth as she sobbed, "It's broken! Ahhh! It's broken!" The tears were already soaking through the daisies on her shirt.

Kyle shoved me with surprising force. "You killed my only sister!"

"Chill out, Kyle!" I barked. "She'll be fine." Of course, I had no idea whether she would be fine. I was still in shock that my kick had actually worked on a human being.

Eric tried to move her again, but Jenna fought him off with her good arm and punched him square in the gut. The other arm hung limp at her side, like a giant mosquito had sucked the life out of it. I couldn't stop staring at it either. I was hypnotized by what I had done and could only hope Jenna wasn't as hurt as it seemed.

And then something strange happened. It makes sense now when I look back at it, but in that moment, it was unexplainable. The air felt heavier. The breeze shifted, and the hair on my arms stood back up. It felt like the space around me was getting smaller and smaller, and there was nothing I could do about it. Whatever it was, it was a dark feeling that made me feel cold and helpless. I wrapped my arms around my body to keep the warmth from escaping me. Something was different about me, but I couldn't peg it.

"Matt? Matt!" Eric yelled. "Snap out of it! What are you doing just standing there?"

I shook my head, and the cold, dark feeling vanished. Eric recovered quickly from the punch to the stomach and ran inside the house to get his parents. By the time they got to Jenna, she had cried out all her tears and had no power left to yell. The only noise that filled the void of Jenna's screams were Kyle's words as he ran away.

"You broke my sister's collarbone! You're going to be in so much trouble!"

He was right too. As soon as Mom and Dad got home, they sat me on the living room couch and let me have it. The punishment was gruesome for any eleven-year-old.

"No more watching fighting shows on TV. No Saturday cartoons. No more practicing karate moves with Eric—*for three months*," Dad listed.

"You can't be serious, Dad!" I pleaded.

"Do I look like I'm kidding?!" he yelled. Dad's face was frozen, his eyes locked into the middle of my face. His chest was heaving up and down, and smoke was coming out of his nostrils.

I decided it was best not to respond.

Basically, anything I liked with fighting or wrestling was not allowed in our house for a long time, and that stunk. But it was nothing compared to what the Curse would punish me with later.

You see, sometimes, life has its own way of handing out punishment, and it doesn't follow a rule book. I had broken my first bone—well, Jenna's first bone—and life was going to give me a dose of my own medicine. Correction: life was going to give me *doses* of my own medicine.

This is the beginning of how life got back at me and cursed me with ten broken toes by the end of sixth grade.

CHAPTER 2
THE MONSTER

My fighting move on Jenna was one of the most incredible things I'd ever done, but Jenna didn't think so. She never appreciated the art of a good karate chop or a double high kick, so breaking her collarbone wasn't going to help her lack of love for martial arts. I visited her in the hospital with my mom that evening while she waited for a doctor to run some kind of extra test, but only because Mom made me.

"Hi Jenna," Mom said while setting a vase of flowers on the side table of the hospital bed. "How are you feeling today? Any better?"

"Um, okay, I guess. Everyone is really nice here, but I can't move. It's boring," Jenna shrugged with her one good shoulder.

Mom pushed back Jenna's hair and began her sympathy speech. "Oh, we all feel so bad for you, sweetie. Your summer shouldn't have to be like this. We wish there was something we could do. Isn't that right, Matt?"

I was still standing at the doorway, looking in the mirror. Mom had tried straightening my hair with a comb right before to look good for the hospital visit. She had said it would work, but it hadn't. My brown mop-looking hair shot out in every direction and hid the freckles on my face. Dad calls my hair the Monster because it looks like it's trying to attack anyone who approaches it. He thinks he's funny.

"I said, we *all* wish there was something we could do. Right, Matt?"

I snapped from my trance and nodded. I had nothing else to say.

On the way back home, I told Mom about *the feeling* that had come over me the day before, but she didn't get it.

"It was weird, Mom. It was such a dark feeling. It made me feel cold and small. Even Eric had to yell to get my attention. What do you think it was? A ghost?" I asked.

"Don't be ridiculous, Matt. You know what that feeling was."

"What was it?"

"That's guilt, honey. And shame. You feel bad because you hurt Jenna. That's all. And you should too. It's perfectly natural to feel that way."

I don't think she quite understood what I was trying to tell her. I knew what guilt was; I'd lied to my parents plenty of times. But guilt was nothing like what I'd felt when I broke Jenna's collarbone. Something felt . . . *off*. Different. It was attached to me. Since Mom didn't have an answer, I just tried to ignore *the feeling*.

When she got home from the hospital, Jenna didn't even look in my direction as she got out of the car and then locked herself inside the house. I didn't know what else to do, so I made her a card. I was too scared to give it to her, though, so I figured Kyle would pass it along for me. I found him dancing in his yard with an army action figure.

"Could you please give this to Jenna?" I asked politely.

"Why? What is it?" Kyle said, already sounding annoyed.

"A card."

He tore the letter open to read it. "Are these supposed to be animals you drew for her? And is that an elephant or a giant rat?"

"I tried my best, okay?!" I defended. I wasn't a great artist, but it looked good to me.

"And what's this?" Kyle asked. "You wrote, *I'm sorry for knocking you down with my awesome karate move.* How is that going to make her feel better?!"

Maybe it wasn't a good idea to make her a card, but I stuck to my plan. "I don't know. Can you just give it to her for me? Please?"

"Why should I?" he asked. "She hates you now."

"Just do it, Kyle. It won't hurt anybody," I insisted.

I watched as Kyle took it inside, but I didn't wait for him to return. I had soccer practice that night, and I didn't want to be late. If I was, Coach Cup would make me pay for it.

Coach Cup was a grumpy, mean, and eccentric old man. He never talked at a normal level. I don't think he could, actually. Instead, he just yelled and screamed, and none of it ever made sense. Like the one time he told our team that if we lost the next game, the soccer balls "wouldn't be our friends anymore."

That night, Coach made us run for the entire practice for losing the last game. Eric got the worst of it too, since he had been the goalie during the loss. He had to hold the push-up position for twenty minutes, and Coach said if Eric's body touched the ground, he would never play soccer again.

By the time practice was finished, Eric couldn't push himself off the ground, and the rest of the team, including me, crawled back home. It was one of the worst practices ever, and I was looking forward to just sitting at home and eating junk food the rest of the night.

Dad had other plans, though.

🔆

"Come on, Dad! Are you serious?" I whined. "I just got done with soccer practice. I'm beat!"

"Sorry, buddy. It's your turn to walk the dog. Your brother did it yesterday and the day before," Dad said calmly while turning the volume up on the TV.

"Ugh! She can just run around outside by herself, Dad. She doesn't need me!" I insisted.

"Matt, she'll run away like last time. Don't act like you don't know. It'll take you thirty minutes, and you'll be done before you know it." The volume was all the way up on the television now, so I knew the conversation was over. I had lost. I accepted my defeat.

I hated walking our dog, Nala. I loved her to death, but walking her was a real chore. Our family had just adopted her a few months ago, and she'd quickly transformed from a cute, adorable puffball into a muscular, full-grown mutt who wouldn't listen. It wasn't Nala's fault she wouldn't do anything we said, though—it was ours. When my family adopted her from the shelter, the worker had said we needed to start training Nala immediately or else she would become a wild, disobedient pet. My parents took this very seriously, so they scheduled what they called "Nala Training Days" for Nala, Elliott, and me.

Our job was to go through an annoyingly long instructional book and train Nala to do things like sit, roll over, and fetch stuff. We were supposed to do Nala Training Days every day for the first month, but we didn't. Not because we didn't want to but because she was too cute! Elliott and I could never focus. Her thick, soft white coat made her look like a giant cotton cloud with feet. Anytime we got close to her, she'd jump up and down, bark in a high-pitched squeak, and rub her face in the tall grass, anticipating playtime. We couldn't resist.

Instead of training, we sat on the ground beneath the shade of our large sap tree and wrestled her. We'd giggle and laugh as she snipped at our toes, ran in circles, and jumped on our laps for hours. When Mom and Dad would ask how training was going every afternoon, Elliott and I made up stories like, "Nala can play dead and walk on her hind legs and even roll over!" They believed us at first, but they caught on to the lies soon enough.

We were outside one afternoon, and Elliott was bragging up a storm to Dad. "Nala can jump! She can flip! She can open doors! She can—"

"Then show me," Dad interrupted. "Show me one of these tricks."

"Ugh . . . okay," Elliott hesitated. He pointed at our dog. "Nala, sit!"

Nala ate some grass.

"Ugh . . . I meant roll over!" Elliott tried again.

Nala licked her paws.

"Nala, stop it!" he yelled.

Nala ran off to the neighbor's house.

Since we had messed up Nala Training Days, Elliott and

I had to take turns walking her around for exercise in our neighborhood, which was a mile-and-a-half-long loop. We lived way out of town in the country, so I didn't mind the scenery at all during these walks. It was a peaceful place with trees that lined the street, blocking most of the houses from view. I liked the feeling of being swallowed by the surrounding trees and mountains, but it was hard enjoying it with Nala always trying to chase a squirrel or take a leak.

That night I was definitely not in the mood to walk either. Coach Cup had destroyed us during practice, and my legs felt as if they were still running between the goal posts, and they throbbed with each step I took.

I moved past Dad and opened the door to the garage. My legs didn't like moving and creaked in unison with the steps. How was I going to make it around the neighborhood with two sore legs? It would take way longer than thirty minutes to walk it—maybe two hours if I was lucky.

I hobbled to the shelf in the back of the garage and grabbed Nala's blue leash from the tool kit. As I turned toward the back door, I accidently kicked something out from beneath the shelf and into the light of the doorway. It was one of Elliott's rollerblades.

I didn't see an angel that night, but there must have been one in the garage, because those rollerblades were a miracle in disguise. I thought, *If I can squeeze those rollerblades on, Nala could pull me around the block instead! I won't have to walk at all! In fact, I bet if Nala runs fast enough, I can get around the loop in under fifteen minutes!*

Nala must have heard me hit the rollerblades, because she came running into the garage and tilted her head.

"Ha!" I smirked. "Looks like you and I are going to get done a little earlier than usual."

I had to pinch my toes together really tight, but I got into those rollerblades. I stood up from the concrete and slowly rolled my feet back and forth, back and forth, to test them out. Not bad. Despite Elliott always leaving them out in the rain, they felt pretty good. I grabbed Nala by the neck and clipped the leash onto her harness. It was testing time.

I knew Nala would try to take off running right away, so I made sure that one foot was on the brake and the leash was tied to one of my wrists. She tried dragging me for a few feet, but I stood my ground and didn't move. Cleary, she didn't understand we were attached, and she tilted her head like she was asking me a question. But looking cute wasn't going to get her out of this brilliant plan.

"Nala, heel!" I commanded.

She looked back at me and tried to run harder, but I didn't give in to that and dug the brake of the rollerblade into the garage floor.

"Give it up, girl!" I laughed. "I am not falling for your dog tricks."

After realizing that dragging me wasn't an option, Nala began to walk, and our journey began. I didn't have to move a muscle! As long as I kept my legs straight and steered with the leash, it was a smooth ride. We gained speed and zipped past trees so fast that they blurred into one color of brownish green. I was in complete control. Nala didn't seem to mind, either, and I began to think that this could be our new relationship: Nala pulling *me* instead of me pulling *Nala*.

After only ten minutes, we rounded the final corner of the block and started to head back to the house. I was so proud. I chuckled a little at the thought of Elliott having to walk Nala for thirty minutes when it had taken me only ten. It was my secret, and I would never—

The leash jerked. My arms went forward . . . and my chest smacked the ground. **SMACK!** Then, *the feeling* came back. That dark-cold feeling that I had felt when I'd broken Jenna's collarbone.

"Nala, knock it off!" I rubbed my hands together to get the dirt off. "Are you trying to break the leash? C'mon! Stop it!" I screamed.

Wrong command. With my arms still stretched forward, I picked my face off the concrete just in time to see a brown squirrel run across the street. Without hesitation, Nala charged after it, and it was like I wasn't even attached to her. She dragged me with such speed that I could feel my soccer jersey slowly tear apart underneath my chest within a matter of seconds. She pulled me past one driveway, then another, and then another! I tried to get the leash off my wrist, but I had no control.

Nala swiveled into a sharp turn as the squirrel evaded her, but my body didn't follow Nala's path. I spun and logrolled over and over and over again, the rollerblades taking turns smacking the street. I felt one rollerblade explode as it hit the ground and bounced back up, sending plastic pieces flying into the air, and exposing my toes. Miraculously, my elbows and knees landed in some soft grass, but my foot wasn't so lucky. It came back down to earth, toes first, and smashed the pavement. **CRACK!** A sharp pain raced up the outside of my right foot, and at the same time I heard the **SNAP** of Nala's leash as I toppled into a small ditch. Her barking slowly disappeared as she chased the squirrel down the street.

I was furious but couldn't yell because my foot was pulsing with pain and my body felt like it was on fire. I sat up and focused my eyes on my chest. It looked like a burned hamburger, covered with specks of blood, little pebbles, and dirt. My soccer jersey was no longer recognizable, either, and it covered only my back.

I rolled over to examine my foot. The rollerblade really had exploded, and my toes stuck out through the top like a weed. I pulled my leg closer to get a better look and see where the throbbing pain was coming from. Most of the toes looked okay, some scratches here and there, but the pinky toe was bent in the opposite direction. It was clearly broken. As soon as my brain realized what was going on, a wave of overwhelming pain sent my body into the shakes, and I started to feel really, really dizzy.

And at that same moment, *the feeling* came back—the feeling of cold, dark nothingness. It made my lungs heavy and my shoulders tight. It was summer, but I could see my own breath clouding my vision of the street. I figured I was in shock from the broken toe, but *the feeling* lingered. I managed to stand up and stagger back home, but I cried as soon I got back inside.

Dad saw me walk in and didn't say a thing. I didn't give him a chance. My face found its way into his shoulder, and I let out a few sobs.

"What's this?" Dad said. He pointed to my toe sticking out of rollerblades. I had left them on.

"Oh boy, Matt, that looks broken," he continued and led me to the bathroom.

While Dad cleaned me up with a wet towel, he explained that the only way to fix a broken toe was to tape it to the toe next to it.

"We'll need to use a couple strips of tape and wrap them a few times," he instructed and began moving the roll around my toes.

"Oww! Dad! That hurts so much! Shouldn't I go to the hospital or something?" I asked. "I mean, it's broken!"

Dad didn't seem concerned and laughed. "You think they make casts small enough for your toes? They'll just tell you to stay off your feet."

It made me laugh a little, but it still hurt. Dad said that for three weeks, my pinky toe would be happily tapped to its neighbor toe.

Dad never told me that rollerblades and walking the dog had been a dumb idea. He didn't have to—I should have known better. And I couldn't be mad at Nala either. She didn't listen, but at least she was loyal. She showed up shortly after I got home, with that tongue-out smile she always does, and kept me company on the couch the rest of the night while I iced my foot and watched TV. I think she felt guilty for dragging me all the way home and breaking toe number one.

And if Nala's guilt felt anything like mine for Jenna, then we both were feeling pretty miserable.

Right before I went to bed that night, my brother said something strange while we brushed our teeth.

"Looks like life got back at you," he said as he spit into the sink. "It's still not fair, though, since you only have a broken toe and Jenna has a broken collarbone."

I didn't feel like comparing injuries. "I still feel bad about that, okay? Don't bring it up." I turned off the faucet and went to my room.

I had a hard time sleeping that night. I couldn't lie on my chest because of the cuts, and even the bed sheets hurt my toe when they hit it. But that wasn't what kept me up all night: Elliott's words gave me the creeps.

I tried to shake it off, but I couldn't get the question out, and I let it run over and over in my head: what would it take to make Jenna and me even?

Now that I look back on it, even if I would have known the answer to that question, it wouldn't have saved me from everything else that happened later that year. My course was set, and there was no way to get out of it. The Curse already had me by the toes, literally, and it was plotting its next move. I just didn't know it yet.

CHAPTER 3
THE PURPLE GRAPE

No matter what happens, Sundays feel the same.

You wake up a little later than usual, eat some breakfast while watching television, and then spend the rest of the day thinking about how Monday is coming in less than twenty-four hours. In the summer, it means chores. In the school year, it means school. Of course, you could *try* to get your mind off it by going swimming, catching frogs, watching a movie, or—my personal favorite—eating a gallon of ice cream. But no matter how much fun you cram into the afternoon, it will never be as good as Friday or Saturday, because those days are limitless. You can do anything you want, without a care in the world. But not Sundays. They stink. And since my toe was broken, it made everything feel that much worse.

On Sunday, I went on errands with Mom all over town, like grocery shopping at Pauly's Marketplace, and that's where my embarrassment began.

"Mom, please don't make me," I begged. "I'll just sit at the front of the store or something, okay?"

"Don't make this a public battle. Your dad and Elliott went hiking together. I can't leave you by yourself in your condition, so don't complain," Mom insisted.

I sighed. If Mom was making me go to the grocery store, at least I'd get some fun out of it. I climbed into the attachment made for little kids on the shopping cart and just barely fit.

Going grocery shopping, for Mom, was like social hour at church. Mom knew everyone, and we saw everyone that day.

"Susan! Is that you? Come say hi to Matt and me!" Mom waved excitedly.

And then, not two seconds later, "Paula? Bring your boys over here and say hi to Matt!"

And another two seconds. "Rachel?! So good to see you! Bring your daughter over here and let's catch up!"

At home, things weren't much better either. Instead of sitting in a cart, I was sitting on the couch. Or sitting in a chair. Or sitting next to Elliott as he chewed cereal in that slow-motion cow-chew he always does. Ew.

But Sunday, after almost a week riding in shopping carts by myself, Mom said I could invite Eric while we ran errands, so at least there would be company. The next day I called Eric and asked whether he would come with Mom and me. Mom said she would take us out for ice cream since it was so hot, so Eric practically ran over when I told him.

We slid into my parents' maroon car and were greeted by the hot, moist air trapped inside. Gross. It was like the inside of a dog's mouth. At 9:00 in the morning, the temperature was already pushing 90 degrees. After only ten minutes of driving, the shirt on my back was soaked with sweat, and it stuck to the car seat as we weaved in and out of traffic. I cranked the air-conditioning, hoping that by the time we reached town, the sweat stains would disappear and I wouldn't smell like a wet gym bag.

We came to the next streetlight, and traffic was stopped in all directions. I figured there was an accident and couldn't contain my excitement that running errands with Mom might be finally over for the day.

"Yes! Maybe there's a fire!" I shouted.

"Or a broken fire hydrant!" Eric joined.

"Or a spilled vegetable truck! Or a—"

"You both stop it!" Mom lectured. "Someone could be seriously injured up there."

I hate seeing people in danger or getting hurt. But accidents are like watching volcanoes. You never want to be in one, but they are awesome to look at. Smashed cars, things on fire, and sirens are cool. I admit it.

I expected to see a wreck or maybe, if I was lucky, a huge fire. My guess was wrong, though—not even close.

We got into the next lane and slowly drove all the way up to the white-striped crosswalk. Instead of a flaming car or a firetruck, standing in the middle of the intersection was an old lady.

Curly hair shot out from beneath her purple hat, and she waddled her feet like a penguin. She was wearing purple shoes that matched her purple pants, which matched her purple shirt and purple purse.

Eric loved the view. "Dude! Haha! She looks like a walking grape!" he pointed out.

"Yeah!" I laughed. "Like a smooshed grape you don't want to eat!"

As we exchanged jokes, she paced back and forth between the lights, stopping all traffic from moving. If the light turned green for one row of cars, she would walk in front of them. If the light turned green for another row, she walked in front of them.

The other drivers at the intersection were being polite, and no one honked. Still, though, she was blocking traffic in all directions. After a few more minutes of watching the old grape lady, I was sick of it.

"Go around her or something, Mom. This is ridiculous," I said. "We'll never move!"

"Just simmer down and practice being patient," Mom encouraged me.

"Ugh. She is slowing everyone down!" I moaned and folded my arms across my chest.

My patience had run out. I was tired of waiting, tired of her blocking us. My toe hurt, and I wanted ice cream. My sweat was now covering my entire shirt, and Eric and Mom were making annoying comments like:

"Matt, you sure are sweaty, dude."

"Just a little longer …"

"Matt, did you put deodorant on this morning? You reek! Haha!" Eric laughed.

"Matt, just be patient; she's old!" Mom lectured.

Well too bad. Her time was up.

The old grape lady began to shuffle through traffic and onto the crosswalk in front of our car. This was my chance, my one opportunity to get her off the road and out of my way. I waited until she was right in front of the car. Then, with both hands, I jumped in front of Mom almost as if she weren't sitting there and slammed the car horn: ***BEEP! BEEP! BEEEEEEEEEEEEEEEP!***

"Matt! Get back in your seat! What are you thinking?!" Mom yelled, but I was focused on the lady.

She stood there, no reaction, right in front of us. After a few moments, the old grape lady turned, her faded but sparkly purple jacket reflecting some of the sun into my eyes. The rays of light outlined her frail, thin figure and revealed her face, which was all pushed close together. Time had made her shrink in size.

As she turned, her head bent backward as she inhaled a large gulp of air.

"What is she doing?" Eric asked. "Is she all right?"

Then, in one swift motion, she whipped her head forward and launched a huge, wet, slimy spit toward the windshield of our car.

I watched it in slow motion as it splattered itself onto the hood, covering the car in a dark yellowish paste. The droplets bounced and slid their way to the windshield. Even though I was protected by glass, I yelled, "LOOK OUT!" and ducked for protection from the flying globs.

I would like to tell you I did something about this. I would like to tell you I got out of the car and made her apologize and clean it up. But I can't tell you those things, because they didn't happen. Instead, I sat in my seat. I mean, what would *you* do if an old lady spit on your car? Stuff like this doesn't happen every Sunday, so my list of options was kinda thin.

I picked my head up from behind the dashboard of the car and looked for signs of another possible attack. Would she throw her purple purse? Kick our bumper? Lick the tires?

My eyes darted back and forth scanning the area, preparing for anything that the old grape lady might do next.

But nothing ever came. She was gone. You know what wasn't? *The feeling.* It surrounded me for just a second and then disappeared before I could focus in on it. Why was it showing up now?!

I sat up straight, aware that I could be presenting a larger target for the old grape lady, but I took a chance. I spun around. Eric's hands were covering his pimpled face. Apparently, he was as freaked out as I was.

"Eric," I whispered, "I think it's over. She's gone."

"No way, man. I'm not sitting up. There is no way I am going to get drool on me," he muttered.

Eric's face told me he was serious. He was like stone

and not going to move anytime soon. I totally forgot about Mom too. I looked over, and she was smiling a little bit. It was the type of smile you make when you're not sure what else to do. A little smirk, showing no teeth. It looked very uncomfortable.

Her voice suddenly broke the silence. "Well, that was certainly interesting, wasn't it?" She laughed. She pushed her hair back and continued. "I guess we are lucky we don't have a convertible or we'd all be slimy!"

Eric and I both started laughing.

I took one last look in the rearview mirror, and with no sign of the old grape lady, Mom put the car in drive, and we made our way down the street.

For the rest of the day, it was all the three of us could talk about. The whole event distracted me from my toe, which had been pulsing with pain since the morning. Altogether, it was one wild afternoon, and since that day, I always make sure to keep my eyes open, because you never know what could happen on a Sunday. I mean, come on. An old lady spitting on your car?! Who else on earth can say they've had that happen to them?

Nobody can. Just me! Which is why you have to pay attention on Sundays. You could be the one with your own unique—and gross—story.

Why tell the story of the old grape lady, you ask? Well, let's just say this wasn't the last encounter we would have. The Curse had a plan for that too.

CHAPTER 4
MOVING STONES

Toward the end of June, toe number one healed and I was able to go back to a normal summer. By that time, I'd used over two rolls of athletic tape, one small tube of some goopy medicine that Mom said was supposed to help with pain, and countless buckets of ice to make the healing go faster, and it paid off. It looked like a brand-new toe, straight as an arrow.

"Looks better," Elliott said as I removed the last piece of tape. "Too bad you're going to break nine more."

"What's with you and your obsession with my toes? Mind your own business," I barked.

"I'm just sayin' I think you're gonna break more."

"Just stop moving your mouth and hand me that rake."

Elliott's words were easy to shake off, but *the feeling* wasn't. It hadn't left since I'd broken my toe. It wasn't as overwhelming as it had been that first day, but I still felt it. It wasn't painful, just uncomfortable, like when you have a rock in your shoe or your sock is on backward. Anyways, there was nothing I could think of to help, except stay busy.

Besides, the end of June also meant something else: finding a job. You see, most incoming sixth graders got to spend their summer goofing off every day of the week, but not me. Mom and Dad were the only parents who believed summer was a time to learn responsibility and hard work, which was bogus. All three Monkling kids (Eric, Jenna, and Kyle), on the other hand, never had to work. They got to do whatever they wanted all summer long. Ugh. Not fair. Not fair at all.

Elliott and I *used* to do yard work for our neighbor Mr. Parcy every year. But last summer we messed the job up big-time. Elliott forgot to water the garden four days in a row, and all of Mr. Parcy's plants died. Tomatoes, chili peppers, corn—everything in that garden dried up and crinkled in the heat. Elliott would have been the only one fired, except I made a big mistake too.

Mr. Parcy had a massive, fancy push mower. It was a top-of-the-line model, and he took care of it like it was part of his family. He washed it every day, waxed it, and even gave it a fresh coat of green paint one summer. Sometimes if I snuck up on him, I'd catch him talking to it.

"Do you like that new coat of paint? I bet you do. Are you ready to cut some grass? I bet you are." He'd pat the top like it was the head of a horse. "Oh, my sweet little baby tracker, you do such a nice job cutting the grass!"

I really hope I don't start talking to my lawn mower when I'm that age.

It was his precious toy, and he loved it, but he couldn't push it anymore because of his lower-back problems. So he taught me how to do it. The first few times I mowed his lawn, he walked right behind me the whole time, barking orders like a drill sergeant, making sure I didn't mess up.

"Turn now, Matt!" he'd order. "Pivot 45 degrees. Turn now! Pay attention!"

After a while, he trusted me to do it on my own. But he'd later regret that decision.

The lawn mower was fancy, all right, but best of all it was superfast. Sometimes I would have to lean sideways as I curved and cut my way through the lawn to make sure I didn't tip over. It was awesome having that much power. I was a professional Indy lawn mower racer.

The day after Elliott killed the garden, I went too fast. I lost control quickly and hit the sidewalk. The crash bent the lawnmower blade and took a chunk out of the sidewalk. Thankfully, I wasn't hurt, but Mr. Parcy fired me the next day—without pay. Now he would have to find someone else to do his stupid yard work.

This summer, Dad found us this part-time job with Mr. and Mrs. Klinkle, an old couple who had just moved in on the other side of the block, so at least we didn't have to search for a new job by hanging up embarrassing flyers. The Klinkles had told Dad they needed some help in the backyard, and he quickly volunteered us.

"Hurry up, boys, or you're going to be late. Don't make me look bad!" Dad yelled from his office.

"I know, I know, Dad! Back off already," I moaned. I was already bummed about working, and my summer job hadn't even started yet.

"Matt, be nice," Mom interjected. "They are very special people who need kind people like you to help them around the house."

Mom saying "special" about older people usually meant they were picky and rude. I was not looking forward to meeting the Klinkle family.

The first day of the job, Elliott and I packed up all we would need into our beat-up wheelbarrow. Shovels, gloves, rakes—we didn't really know what type of work we would be doing, so we grabbed everything we could think of from the garage.

Elliott hopped in the wheelbarrow too, and since he didn't weigh much, I pushed him and the rest of the stuff toward the Klinkles' house.

We passed the Monklings' house on our way there, and it made me think about Jenna.

I hadn't spoken to Jenna since the karate move, but that didn't mean I wasn't *thinking* about her. I had no idea what to say! Plus, would *you* want to see the person who ruined your entire summer?!

I tossed off the feeling of guilt and continued to push the rusty, filled-to-the-top wheelbarrow into the Klinkles' driveway. Elliott enjoyed the ride and begged me to go around the block again. After thinking about Jenna, I was in a bad mood, so I just tipped the wheelbarrow on its side and dumped Elliott out with the rest of the stuff on the driveway. He'd be fine.

While he sat in the pile of shovels and cried, I walked up the red stairs and across the porch and knocked on the door.

"Be right there!" said a low, booming voice. I could feel the voice echoing deep in my stomach, a low rumbling. As the footsteps came closer to the door, the porch shook a little and made my bony knees buckle beneath my shorts.

The door flung open, and my eyes widened. Standing in the doorway was Mr. Klinkle. His body took up the entire door, and I couldn't even see inside the house! I stood there, basking in his shadow. He was the TALLEST man I had ever seen.

He was tall, all right, but round too, which made him like one of those bears right before hibernation. His face was wide, and so was his bald white head, with a few stray brown hairs sticking out from the back.

In the back, I heard Elliott chirp up. "Whoa" was all he could get out.

"It's Matt and Elliott, right? Bring your stuff to the back," Mr. Klinkle sputtered, and he slammed the door in my face.

I turned to Elliott. He was still staring at the door like he had seen a ghost or something. I guess he was as shocked by Mr. Klinkle as I was. I tried to bring Elliot back to reality and poked his shoulder.

"Elliott. Are you okay?" I gave him another poke.

He slowly turned his head toward me and smiled. "Matt, that is the tallest human of all the humans I have ever seen in my whole entire life! Did you see him? Did you?!"

"Yeah, I saw him. He is kind of hard to miss," I giggled.

"I didn't even know it was possible to grow that tall," Elliott said, looking back at the doorway. "Can I get that tall, Matt?"

"No. Kids who eat cereal like a cow can't grow that tall," I said. "Let's go."

We threw the shovels and rakes back in the wheelbarrow and started walking around the house. It was all white, except for the red porch. When I got home, I could probably make a good model of it if I had enough white bricks.

We reached the back of the house and saw a desert. There was no grass, just a bunch of dirt, weeds, and stones. It was one of the worst yards I had ever seen. You could see the haze of the sun sizzling off it.

"All right. Here is what you need to do," he coughed.

Mr. Klinkle's head was now sticking out of the kitchen window. He pointed. "Take those weeds—pull 'em out. Then I want you to move all those rocks." COUGH. "And stones. If they are bigger than a quarter, they have to be moved out to the driveway." COUGH. "Let me know when you're done."

The blinds in the kitchen went down, and just like that, he was gone.

I scanned the backyard. It was all rock. Some rocks were really small, about the size of a pea, but others were bigger than Elliott's head. Maybe if I had a small army under my command, we could get the job done in a week, but with just Elliott, it would take us months—maybe even the whole summer.

We began lifting rocks and throwing them in the wheelbarrow. After about five minutes, I was already tired and bored, and Elliott was sitting under the shade of the house, taking a break.

"This is more of a curse than your broken toe!" Elliott said, catching his breath.

"Whatever, Elliott. It's not a curse. Get back to work," I grumbled and lodged my shovel back into the earth.

Curse or no curse, it was going to be a long summer moving stones, and it was about to get even worse.

CHAPTER 5
TOE NUMBER TWO

Moving rocks at the Klinkles' stunk. It was the same thing every single day. Find a rock, bend over, pick it up. Find a rock, bend over, pick it up. My back was killing me, and my hands were raw from pulling dirt, weeds, and twigs. Elliott wasn't doing much better and spent a day at home because of the massive blisters on his hands. He was lucky.

I was about to get a break, though. The beginning of July, besides work, also meant soccer tryouts for the Montrose Mountaineers traveling team, and this year tryouts were going to be at Chimney Rock College in Durango, a few hours from my house. I was going to get to stay in a room at the college for a full week! By the end of camp, I would know whether I had made the competitive traveling team. I was finally old enough to join, and I wanted a spot on the team more than anyone else. Only problem was Coach Cup was the new coach of the team.

After church on Sunday (I kept my eyes open for the old grape lady on the way home but didn't see her), Mom, Dad, Elliott, and I packed the car with all my gear for camp. We filled it with shin guards, long socks, protein drinks, granola bars—it was like I was leaving the country!

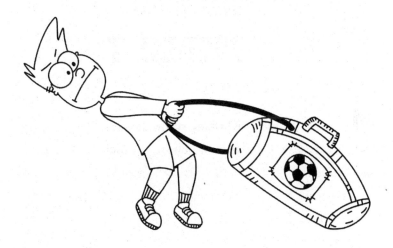

We swung by the Monklings' house and picked up Eric first. He was also hoping to get a spot on the team, and my dream was that both of us would make it. If it came down to a final decision, though, and I had to choose, I decided I would take the last spot instead of Eric. Sorry. Being friends doesn't get you anywhere in the soccer world.

After two hours of driving through the mountains, we arrived at camp. It was a gorgeous campus. It sat on a high green hill that overlooked an old mining town, and you could even see some snow left on the caps of the surrounding mountains. The town looked fake, like the ones you put around a train set. Most of the buildings were either red brick or wood and looked really worn out. Still, I liked the idea that I was in a place that had been around for so many years.

We parked by the entrance and walked past the soccer fields. There were so many of them, and they were already filled with other kids kicking balls back and forth. I couldn't wait to get out there.

"Do you think we can beat them and get on the team?" Eric asked. I could tell he was really nervous, because he kept scratching his head like he always did.

"Duh, Eric. These guys are chumps. We'll walk all over them," I said. I wasn't sure of that, but Eric and I were pretty good, and it would take a lot of talent to make us look bad.

We made our way to the front office and checked in.

"Eric and Matt?" The clerk double-checked. "Well, look at that! You're roommates for the week!"

"Yes!" we said simultaneously. It was comforting knowing I wouldn't have to worry about anyone weird sleeping in my room.

We got our keys and walked with my family to room 180 on the first floor. The room wasn't anything special: a baby-blue carpeted floor with gray brick walls, a bunk bed, a desk with a phone, and two wooden closets for our soccer gear. From our window, you could see the practice fields and the cafeteria building. This would be our home for the next week: this room and the soccer fields.

I hugged my parents goodbye and told Mom I would call her every night. I knew she would like that.

"You promise?" Mom asked. "Because I really want to hear about each practice, the food, the activities, the—"

"Mom, I'll call you," I encouraged. "I will."

"One last thing," Dad chimed in. "Don't worry about making the team. Just focus on each practice session. One step at a time, okay?" He patted me on the shoulder.

"Thanks. I'll try," I shrugged. "Elliott, try to get some work done at the Klinkles' while I'm gone, okay?"

He frowned, waved goodbye, and walked out with my parents. I could tell he was already dreading a week working by himself in the rocky yard.

It wasn't long after my parents left that Coach Cup came into our room. He didn't say "Hi" or "Welcome to camp, boys!" He just threw us each a folder. "Be at the fields by 7:00 a.m. tomorrow or don't show up at all!" he yelled, and slammed the door on his way out.

Eric and I read through our folders, which contained our schedule, eating times, and gear requirements.

By the time I finished reading it all, it was already 8:00 p.m. Eric and I wanted to be prepared for the next day, so we brushed our teeth, got our gear ready for practice, and hit the lights. But Eric had to get something off his chest first.

"I've been meaning to ask you," he said in the dark. "Do you think breaking your toe the day after you broke Jenna's collarbone was a coincidence or a curse?"

"Why do you say that?" I asked. I was sick of his "Curse Theory" already. Maybe he had talked with Elliott.

"I dunno. It's just weird, I guess—you know, that you broke your toe the same week as Jenna's collarbone. Maybe you have the Curse."

"The what?" I asked.

"Never mind. It was . . . nothing. Forget I said anything," Eric said, and he turned over to sleep.

"Whatever. Goodnight, Eric," I said quickly and ended the conversation.

It took me awhile to settle down, but I finally started to drift into sleep. I dozed off wondering what Jenna was doing back home.

Eric and I woke up to the buzzing of two alarm clocks. We rolled out of bed, slipped on our clothes, including the shin guards and cleats, grabbed a protein drink from our bags, and headed out to the fields. The sun was already up, and you could hear the town below the hill coming to life. Cars were humming along, people were getting ready for work, and the old train station whistle was blowing. It gave me a boost of confidence for some odd reason.

By 7:00 a.m. sharp, there were over one hundred boys my age in the center of the field, listening to Coach Cup and his assistant, Coach Reese, describe what would happen over the next few days.

I sat down near the edge of the circle of boys and listened to Coach Cup. He didn't have much to say, just his usual speech.

"You are all going to leave this camp as men! I don't care if you lose a limb in the process. You will live and breathe soccer for the next week and love every minute of it!"

Most of the kids in the circle looked completely terrified, but Eric and I just sat there smirking. Just a regular speech for Coach Cup, and we felt like we had the edge against everyone else at camp.

Assistant Coach Reese took over and talked more about the tryouts. He, at least, seemed normal.

"Each practice, we are going to test your speed, ball control, movement, teamwork, and overall soccer abilities. At the end of the week, more than eighty people will be cut, and only twenty people will make it to the final roster," he announced.

Hearing those numbers made me realize how tough it would be to make the squad, and I swallowed—hard. I looked over at Eric, and he must have been thinking the same thing, because he was scratching his head again.

☀

The first three days of practice weren't too bad. There was a lot of running, which was my best skill, and I made sure to beat people to the ball whenever I had the chance. To make a good impression, I sprinted everywhere I went: the drinking fountain, the bathroom, the sidelines. While everyone else walked, I ran to show off my speed.

I didn't see Eric very much, except at night, but we were both too tired to talk by that time, so we caught up during lunch and dinner each day. Of course, Eric thought he was doing horrible and was sure he would be one of the eighty people cut during tryouts.

"I just don't know, Matt," he mentioned at lunch one day. "These guys are so good! I'm not gonna make it. I should just sit and watch."

So I reminded him about Dad's advice: "Just focus on the practices, Eric. Don't worry about the end of it."

"Okay. Thanks, Matt," Eric said. Dad's words seemed to help a little, but not much. Eric kept twitching.

If he thought days one, two, and three were bad, though, he must have died when we entered day four. Practice was more intense—more running, more passes, more headers. It was almost too much soccer. People were getting hurt, and kids were beginning to get really competitive and mean. During a scrimmage on day four, I bumped into a player on the sideline while I waited my turn to play, and he lost control.

"Hey! Stay out of my way or I'll bust your knees!" His

face was beet red, and his hands were in tight fists. He stepped forward and shoved me in my chest.

"Not if I break your nose!" I yelled. I would have done it too, but Coach Cup was too close, so I just walked away and sat by myself and tried to let my anger cool. I didn't want to blow my chances at making the team because of some fight with a stupid, tall, hairy sixth grader. Everyone was in the same spot, anyway: angry and scared.

After choking down the macaroni and cheese the cafeteria gave us for dinner (the cheese didn't even stick to the noodles), Eric and I walked back to our room. He didn't say it, but I could tell he was going to go to bed as soon as we got back. It was only 7:30, but the idea of sleeping sounded too good to pass up. I didn't bother washing up for bed. Instead, I got in the room, let my body fall on the bed with my feet on the pillow, and dozed off to sleep.

I couldn't have been asleep more than five minutes before I heard pounding on the door.

"Get out here! Let's do this now!" yelled an exhausted but violent voice.

I flipped my feet over the bed and looked up at Eric. He was still asleep. The noise hadn't bothered him at all. If it wasn't for the hair going in and out of his mouth each time he breathed, you'd have thought he was dead.

I opened the door expecting to see Coach Cup, but nope—it was the kid from the scrimmage whom I'd wanted to punch in the face. He was breathing heavily, and his eyebrows were crossed below his fiery red hair.

"I said get out here!" He grabbed my shirt and yanked me into the hallway. Now that we were in the thin brick hallway, his body seemed even bigger than before. I was a mouse compared to him.

"You think you're so good at soccer, don't you? You think you're just the best at everything?" he barked.

"No, but I'm way better than you," I shot back. My mouth said the words without permission from my brain. That was one mistake, and I was about to make two more.

"Fine! We'll play right now in this hallway!" he said and picked up the soccer ball next to his feet. "If I get the ball past you, I get a point. You get it past me, *you* get a point. First one to three wins. Got it?" He was holding a soccer ball above his head now like it was some sort of prize. He was ready to play too. He was wearing shin guards and tennis shoes, like he'd planned this all out, maybe to try to embarrass me in front of his friends. Whatever. I'd seen him play earlier that day, and he was less than perfect.

"Fine," I said. I flipped my socks off so I could play in bare feet. That was mistake number two.

The small crowd of smelly, grungy boys gathered around behind us. The redhead started with the ball at his feet and took a run to see whether he could scare me away. I jumped to the side and snatched the ball with my right foot, kicking it down the hallway past him. Score 1–0.

The redheaded ogre stomped his feet. "C'mon! Gimmie that ball!"

He tried the same thing as before, running at me full speed with the ball. I guess he thought that since he was so big, I would eventually move, but I didn't. Again, I whipped my bare foot in front of the ball and made it come to a dead stop, tripping the boy as I skimmed the ball to my other foot and kicked it down the hall for another point. Score 2–0.

"Rrrrrr! Gimmie that ball again!" he screamed.

"Yeah, right!" I laughed. "You started with it twice; now it's my turn to start with the ball! Nice try!" I was one point away from making him look like a complete fool in front of his friends. He was nothing more than a big set of feet with red hair. I grabbed the ball and placed it on the floor in front of me. I was going to kick that ball so hard that if he tried to stop it, it would knock him backward.

I took a couple steps back and ran at the ball with every

ounce of energy I had left. I swung my right leg back, closed my eyes, and launched my foot forward to kick the ball.

That was mistake number three.

I told you my best skill in soccer was running. My worst skill, though, was shooting. I completely missed the ball, and my foot continued its path straight into the brick wall of the hallway. **CRACK!**

I felt a rush of cold blood go to the front of my face. My other leg went limp, and I collapsed to the ground.

"Whoa! Nice shot!" someone yelled.

I could hear laughter around me, but I couldn't get my eyes to focus on anything. My entire body felt cold and burning hot at the same time. Every breath I took made it different. Hot air, then cold air—my senses were all scattered, and my body was in shock.

And then *the feeling* came.

This time it stayed. It wound its way around my leg, traveled up my back, and touched the top of my head like a python wrapping around its prey.

I made myself get to my knees and pulled myself back into room 180. I could still hear the bully out in the hallway.

"We ain't done yet! Get back out here! I can beat you!" he yelled.

The feeling continued to wrap around me. The air was heavy, and the room was spinning.

That's the last thing I remembered before everything went black.

CHAPTER 6
COACH REESE

I woke up to Eric's face over my head, saying my name over and over.

"Matt. Matt! What are you doing on the floor? Get up— you're going to be late! Get up!" he said as I shook my head.

I looked around the room, and he was right. I wasn't in bed. I was smack in the middle of our room, lying on the floor.

"Matt, you need to get your cleats on quick or else you'll be—" Eric gasped. "Whoa! What happened to your foot?!"

Eric's sudden change in expression made me sit up. He was staring at my right foot, scratching the side of his head. Not a good sign.

I followed his gaze and looked at my foot. The big toe, the father of all the other toes, was swollen and purple. It had grown so much overnight that it was pushing the toe next to it out of the way, making room for its enormous new size.

"Does it . . . hurt?" Eric asked.

"Ugh, not too bad. It's throbbing a little," I replied.

"I'll help you up. Here." Eric grabbed my arm and hoisted me to my feet. I didn't think about not letting the big toe touch the ground, and I put all my weight on it. What I got was an immediate pulse of sharp pain, and Eric had to catch me before I fell to the ground. He managed to get me to the edge of the bed as I hopped on one foot.

"That's not good, dude. That's two broken toes in a just a few weeks! You must have the Curse! Think you can play on it?" He was still scratching his head.

"The *what*? Curse? What are you talking about?!" I yelled, mocking his guess. "Yeah, right! What do you think, Eric?! Are you serious?! No, I can't play on it! I can barely walk!" I didn't want to be so mean to him, but the words just came out.

"Sorry! I was just trying to help you. Good luck getting to practice, jerk!" Eric grabbed his bag and left the room.

That was the last thing I needed. My one friend at camp was gone and probably hated me on top of it. I had been a jerk to him, but I couldn't control myself. I was so distraught. My toe was broken, and my chances of making the team were gone. All the hard work, the extra running, and the great plays I had made were worthless. All I could do was slump on the floor and cry and wonder what Eric had meant by "the Curse." It wasn't a comforting thought either.

I skipped morning practice and called Mom to tell her what had happened. Between sobs, Mom reminded me it was Friday, the last day of camp, so she would be there in a couple hours after the last practice session. She made sure to say she was proud of me and hung up the phone to go get ready to pick me up.

I skipped lunch that day. I slept for a little while, but most of the time I just stared at the ceiling from the bed. I didn't want to see Eric, Coach Cup, or the red-haired kid. Why bother? Going to practice wouldn't change anything. I didn't want to be at camp anymore; I just wanted to be at home with Nala on the couch like the last time I'd broken a toe.

As I stared at the ceiling, there was a sudden clicking noise. The door opened and in walked Coach Reese, cheerful as always. He carried a much gentler face than Coach Cup and grinned as he walked through the doorway with his clipboard and red bag. Seeing him so happy only made me feel worse.

"How'd you get in?" I sniffed. "The door was locked."

"Oh, ha. *That*," Coach Reese grinned. "I have keys to this entire building. There isn't a door here I can't open."

He was still smiling, but I didn't respond.

"I heard you busted your toe last night," he said. "Is that true? Can I see it?"

I extended my leg from the edge of the bed so he could see it better. I didn't think it was possible, but my toe had gotten bigger since the last time I'd looked at it.

"That's quite the swollen toe, there, Matt. I suppose it's hard to walk on, huh?" Coach asked.

I nodded shamefully, and he continued. "Well, I thought you might like to hear some news, since you didn't make it to practice this morning."

I knew it. I was getting cut for sure.

"Coach Cup and I decided last night that some individuals stood out more than others during the last practice. Some athletes just work a lot harder, and we coaches notice things like that. So instead of waiting for another full day of tryouts, we made our choices for the competitive team last night. You understand, right?"

I sat there. *Just finish this already*, I thought to myself. *Let me go home.*

"That's why Coach Cup and I decided that you need to be on the competitive team, Matt. You worked really hard during practice, and we saw that. You will be a great asset to the team this year."

Huh? I picked up my head. His words didn't seem real.

"But that foot of yours . . . that's going to keep you off the field for a while, so you'll need a temporary replacement, someone who can cover for you while you heal. We'll have to figure that out later, but in the meantime"—Coach Reese motioned toward me—"let's keep this a secret between us, okay? The other boys won't find out whether they're cut till the end of the day."

I was too shocked to be excited. "Okay, sounds good" was all I got out.

"Great, I'll inform your parents when they come this evening. Stay here and rest up, all right, buddy?" He slapped my leg with his clipboard and started walking out the door, but not before I asked one last question.

"Wait. Coach Reese?"

"Yeah?"

"Did Eric Monkling make the team?"

"Eric? No, sorry. He didn't make the cut. Maybe next year," he offered.

My mind raced. "Um, Coach, do you think Eric could be my replacement, just until I get better?"

With his back still turned, Coach Reese leaned on the doorframe and flipped through his clipboard. "I think that might work. Yeah, that should work well. I'll talk with Coach Cup, and I'll tell Eric what we talked about."

I bit my lip and shut my eyes and made one last request. "Actually, don't tell him we talked. I don't want him to know."

"All right," Coach said, "but I am still telling him he is your replacement for the next few games, okay?"

I nodded as he left, closing the door behind him.

I lay in bed the rest of the day, thinking about all the big games I would get to play in during sixth grade. I couldn't get the smile off my face. Dad's advice had worked as usual, and I was going to be part of the team I dreamed about—and so was Eric. Kind of.

But I was worried too. I had broken a second toe, and it made Elliott and Eric's "Curse Theory" seem a bit more realistic. I'd have to ask Eric what he'd meant by "the Curse" the next time I saw him.

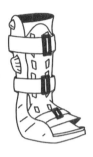

CHAPTER 7
BIG BUBBA

My parents, Eric, and I celebrated a successful week of camp on the way home with a stop by Durango's famous Dotted Parlor. That wasn't Mom's first choice, though. Her first choice was to go to the hospital, but I wanted to celebrate first.

"Matt, we really need to go to the hospital," Mom said as we drove through the town. "We need to get that looked at immediately."

"C'mon, Mom! I'm fine!" I lied. "Plus, Dad even said you don't need to go to the hospital for a broken toe—remember?!"

She didn't respond, which meant I was winning the argument. My toe *did* hurt, but I didn't want anyone to think I couldn't handle it. Plus, I love winning a good argument.

"Please, Mom?" I continued. "There is no way we are driving past Dotted Parlor and not stopping. Seriously, I'm good!"

Mom looked deep into my eyes, then at my toe, then into my eyes again. "Okay," she said hesitantly. "But if you start feeling worse, you tell me right away, okay?"

"Yes!" I cheered. "Let's go!"

The ice cream shop had been around for more than twenty years and boasted over fifty types of different ice cream toppings. I ordered the biggest item I could, the Deluxe Triple Scoop Caramel Blast—with sprinkles. It had been a tough week, and nothing makes a bad memory go away better than a big pile of ice cream—I guarantee it.

My parents' excitement for Eric and me was hidden, though. They were both concerned about my toe, which was now more swollen than before.

"What should we do? Soak it in ice water? I can go get some from the counter," Mom said to Dad.

I poked my toe lightly with my spoon to make sure it was still alive.

"I don't know. It's pretty big," Dad replied. "Your pinky toe didn't scare me too much, but this one is making *me* sick just looking at it, Matt. I think we better go to the doctor after we get home."

Eric seemed to be having a conversation, too—with himself. He kept scratching his head, slower this time than before.

"What if I mess up during the game? What if I cause the team to lose? What if I score in the wrong goal?" he mumbled.

The what-ifs didn't stop from Eric until we got back home. I figured he must be happy to be on the team, and worrying was just his way of showing it. He didn't seem mad at me anymore, either, since he kept asking about my toe between his what-ifs.

We dropped Eric off at his house and unloaded all of his soccer gear and leftover food. As soon as his last bag hit the ground, he ran inside his house yelling, "I made the team! I made the team!"

He didn't bother saying goodbye to us, but I don't think any of us cared. I got back in the car and propped my foot up from the back seat onto the driver's-side armrest. It felt good to get my toe off the ground and let some cool air from the air-conditioning hit it—a small relief from the constant throbbing.

"We're heading to the doctor's after I drop your mom back at home," Dad announced as he put on his seat belt. "I want to make sure you didn't permanently damage that Big Bubba of yours."

"Damage what?" I laughed. "Big who?"

"Yeah, Big Bubba! It's what you call the leader of the pack. Your big toe is the leader of that foot, and you need to get it fixed before you break any others."

Dad seemed to be in an extra-good mood that day, which helped make the process of getting my toe x-rayed much better. At the urgent care, the doctors made me stand up on my bad foot and put all my weight on Big Bubba. It hurt a lot to stand that way, but I didn't cry. I'd done plenty of that back in room 180.

After the last scan, Dad picked me up off the table, threw me over his shoulder, and carried me to the waiting room. It wasn't long before a doctor came out from behind the desk to give us the results. She flipped through a stack of papers in her hand and pulled out a pink form with my name on it. Dad started massaging the back of my neck, which he usually did when he thought I was nervous.

"Well, Matt, your toe is broken," the doctor announced. She waited for my reaction. Did she expect me to be surprised?

"I could have told you that," I muttered.

Dad didn't like my attitude and squeezed the back of my neck to signal me to be more polite.

Dad scratched his head and questioned the doctor. "What type of break is it?"

"It's a hairline fracture," the doctor responded. "Shouldn't take more than three to four weeks to heal. He won't need crutches, but he will need this boot."

I hadn't even noticed the bag she'd brought with her. She took out a gray boot that had cushions all around it and a few Velcro straps. It looked more like a ski boot, except the front of it was missing.

"Try this on for size," she said. "It'll make walking much easier for you."

I raised one eyebrow in a *yeah, right* sort of way and shook my head. This doctor didn't know what she was talking about. How would a ski boot help Big Bubba?

I slipped my foot inside the plastic boot, and Dad adjusted the straps to make sure it was tight but not too tight. The end of the boot was open, and I could see all five toes sticking out. It reminded me of the rollerblade I had destroyed earlier that same summer.

My first two steps were small, because I was expecting the sharp pain from before. To my surprise, the pain wasn't that bad. I tried to jog a little, but the boot was too big, and I tripped over myself.

"Whoa, buddy. Just take it easy," Dad chuckled as he grabbed my arm to stop me from falling. "You aren't ready for soccer just yet."

Dad signed some papers while I fiddled with the straps on the boot in the waiting room. The boot was comfortable, like walking on pillows or wet sand. Hopefully, the three weeks would go quickly.

When we got home, Elliott was waiting for us in the driveway. He must have been working at the Klinkles' that day, because his face was covered in dirt and he was soaking his hands in a bucket of water. At least having a broken toe would get me away from moving stones for a few weeks.

"Have a good time at the Klinkles' house?" I teased.

"I don't want to talk about it," he said, swirling the water.

But I wasn't impressed. "I hope you made progress, because I won't be able to help you again this week."

Elliott noticed the boot and ignored most of what I said. He asked me a ton of questions all at once. "Can you jump with it on? How heavy is it? Can you take it off? Can I wear it? How much was it?"

His eyes were wide with curiosity, so I tried to answer each one. Halfway through, he let out another barrage of questions that I didn't want to answer. He was making me tired with his constant talking.

"Can we just leave the questions for later, Elliott? It's exhausting."

He proudly spat out one last statement: "I guess Eric was right about the Curse, huh?"

I was confused. "Since when did you and Eric start talking?" I probed. "Just drop it. It is not a curse. It's just life, okay? Things just happen."

"I don't think so, Matt. I still think you've got the Curse," he muttered while shaking his head. "You just wait. I bet you'll break another toe before you know it."

I could have argued with him more, but I was already tired enough from the drive. Maybe if I would have continued the conversation, I could have figured out that only one of us would turn out to be right, but I didn't. Instead, I splashed some water from the bucket in his face.

"Matt! Don't!" he yelled.

I turned around to go inside, but my eyes crossed the fence and caught Jenna standing on her back porch. She was just leaning forward, staring at me. Her arm was in a different-colored sling this time, a bright-green one that matched her shirt. Her legs were locked stiff, and her other arm was on her hip. She looked mad. Really mad.

I stuck my arm up in the air and gave a weak wave in her direction.

"Hi, Jenna! How are you feeling?"

"Leave me alone!" Jenna yelled and went back inside.

I don't know what I was hoping for. I looked down at Big Bubba, my hand still in the air. Only a month into the summer and I'd broken three bones—two of mine and one of Jenna's.

I let my arm fall to my side and hobbled my way through the garage and into the living room, trying to think of something else besides broken bones and Jenna. Dad was lying in the middle of the floor, hands behind his head, watching the football game.

Without taking his eyes off the screen, Dad asked, "Well, Matt, how does the toe feel?"

"It hurts a little, but this boot really helps. I bet I could walk around the whole block, no problem!" I exaggerated a little, but I wanted to show Dad I was tough, just like him.

"Great!" Dad said, eyes still on the TV. "Then you can help your brother at the Klinkles' house next week."

"What? Are you kidding?!" I gasped. My bragging had gone too far and, in the end, would set me up for another long, tiring day.

CHAPTER 8
TOE NUMBER THREE

Dad hadn't been kidding, which meant one weekend to rest before going back to the Klinkles' with Elliott. That boot was already causing more pain than it was saving me. I should have asked the doctor for a can't-do-yard-work note when I had the chance.

Luckily, since Mom knew what was coming the next week, she treated me like a king the entire weekend. I got to eat all my favorite meals, watch movies while icing Big Bubba, and even have Eric over for a sleepover Sunday night.

Mom tried something new that night too. "Here you go, boys!" Mom said as she spun a circle on the kitchen floor. "I hope they're good. I tried my best to copy it." She handed us homemade replicas of the Deluxe Triple Scoop Caramel Blast ice cream. They looked exactly like the real thing.

"Mom, this is awesome!" I said. My mouth was already watering from anticipating the caramel on my tongue.

"Yeah, thanks, Mrs. Sprouts," Eric added. "It can't get any better than this."

Well, it could have been better. Her Deluxe Triple Scoop Caramel Blast wasn't nearly as good as the original, but I complimented Mom anyway.

"It's really good. I hope I break another toe so I can have another!" I teased.

Mom and I had a good chuckle, but Eric didn't.

"Matt, that's not funny! You might be cursed, remember? It's not something you can just goof around about!" he warned me.

"Man, I am sick and tired of you and Elliot and your stupid 'Curse Theory,'" I retorted, shoving another spoonful of the ice cream in my mouth. "It's dumb. Where did you come up with that pile of poop?"

"You mean you don't know the legend of the Curse? It's a Montrose legend that's been around for, like, forever!" he said. He was so dumbfounded by my lack of knowledge that he put his ice cream down.

"I guess I don't know. Please—tell me about this *great curse* thing!" I teased. I really didn't care about it, but seeing Eric so flustered was kinda fun.

He moved closer to me, maybe because he was taking it seriously, and continued. "The legend says that if you do something really bad, and I mean *really* bad, then you'll be cursed with the bad act you did!" He seemed so thrilled to finally say the legend out loud that I thought he was going to pee his pants in excitement. "In fact, I heard there was a kid from our school who got it once and never came back to school! They say he decided to stay home . . . forever."

I put a concerned look on my face and acted like I was doing math problems in the air to amuse Eric. "So if I broke Jenna's collarbone, then that means—"

"Then that means the Curse will start breaking your bones too!" Eric yelled.

I couldn't control my straight face anymore and burst out laughing. "That's the stupidest thing I've ever heard! Ha! You can't be serious!"

"I'm just saying," he continued, "if I were you, I wouldn't tempt the Curse to break another one of your toes."

Mom kept her distance and watched from the kitchen. She looked nervous, so I made another joke to lighten the mood. "It's okay, Mom. I don't believe Eric. I still wish I'd break another so I could eat your ice cream."

Eric, on the other hand, just kept shaking his head.

Monday morning, Elliott and I gathered up our supplies and strolled over to the Klinkles'. My boot took most of the pain away from walking, but my toe still throbbed with its own heartbeat.

When we arrived, Mr. Klinkle was sitting alone on his front porch in an old cushioned chair. It was stained from being left out in the weather and creaked each time he rocked back and forth.

Mr. Klinkle's eyes were shut, but he must have heard us coming up the driveway, because he just pointed toward the back of the house. We walked past him and the chair, and I got my view of the yard for the first time in a week. Elliott had worked on it the whole time I was at soccer camp, but I couldn't even tell.

"Sorry, Matt," Elliott said, hanging his head and circling some dirt with his foot. "I tried really hard to finish it."

"It's all right, El; thanks for trying," I said and patted him on the back. "We'll get it done, even with my broken toe."

He laughed and picked up a shovel. For some reason, yard work brought my brother and me closer together. Maybe it was the fact that we were suffering and had only each other to rely on. With Elliott there, the work just didn't seem so bad.

We spent the next five hours hauling rocks out of the Klinkles' backyard and dumping them in the front driveway like Mr. Klinkle asked. We must have moved over fifty wheelbarrow loads that afternoon, and by the time we were done, my arms were noodles and my boot had a thick layer of mud caked on it. The boot did its job and kept my toe from hurting, but now the rest of my body ached as we gathered our supplies to finish the day.

When Elliott and I got home, we fell into the living room—Elliott in the chair closest to the television and me on the couch. Mom already prepared lunch; she had to practically open our mouths to get the food in since we were so tired. We sat in the same place for the next two hours, watching silly cartoons, sleeping, and nibbling on gummy bears to regain our strength.

Dad got home from work about the time we finished the bag of candy, and he looked just as tired as us.

"Guess what I saw today," Dad said as he plopped down his lunch pail next to the door. There was heavy sarcasm in his voice, which meant one of us must have done something very wrong.

"What?" Elliott and I said it at the same time.

Dad continued with his sarcasm. "I saw eight huge piles of steaming poop in the front yard." His sarcasm began to increase. "What a great present to come home to after a long day of work! Whose turn is it to pick up after Nala?"

Elliott and I glared at each other.

Dad was getting mad—and fast. "Well, figure it out by the time I get back in here!" he yelled. "I'm going to shower."

For the next five minutes while Dad showered, Elliott and I engaged in one of the worst screaming matches we'd ever had. It was a full-out verbal war. I lashed an artillery of personal insults, while Elliott used the volume of his voice to try to win. We were at the edge of our seats, and neither of us was going to back down.

"You do it, Matt! It's your turn this week!"

"Yeah, right, Elliott! I've done it three weeks in a row. Get out there and do it yourself!"

"It's your turn! I'm telling Dad!"

"Not if I tell him first, you little snot!"

Elliott and I never hit each other. In fact, we'd never been in a physical fight before, but I was ready for today to be the first one. So much for the brother bonding we'd done earlier. Third graders can really test your patience, and Elliott was just asking for a kick to the stomach.

When Dad walked in, we were still yelling. I was thinking of what move I should pull on Elliott when Dad cut us off. He was standing in front of the laundry room in his athletic shorts, hair still wet, without a shirt. His face was red, and his muscles were tense.

"Matt and Elliott, I told you that you needed to . . ." Dad tried to interject, but we overpowered him.

"Daaaaaad! It's Matt turn!"

"No, Dad! It's Elliott's turn! He's a liar!"

"Be quiet, Matt!"

"Dad! It's his turn! He never—"

Dad's body stayed facing the door, and he let out a heavy sigh. Then in a deep, slowly controlled voice, he yelled, "Figure it out NOW!"

Suddenly, it became a race to see who could get outside first. Elliott leaped in front of the couch and jetted out the sliding glass door. I followed as quickly as I could, stumbling over my boot on the way out.

Elliott had already grabbed me a shovel by the time I got to the garage, and we both frantically searched the front yard for Nala's poop. There were no words spoken between us. Dad rarely yelled at us, ever. And hearing him raise his voice like that made me feel, well, not great.

The shovel filled up quickly, and I couldn't fit any more poop on. Nala must have eaten a lot that week, because the piles were so massive it was like trying to get gum off the carpet. Making it worse, every single pile looked fresh and smelled of rotten fish. I needed a break before I threw up.

"I'm going to throw this out. I'll be back in a minute," I mumbled to Elliott. He wiped some of his tears away and kept scooping.

I took the walk past the backyard to the pasture to throw the poop in the burn pile. Our yard was long and wide and mostly filled with tall, dead grass. We never used it, though, because it shared a back fence with Farmer Jed. He was a sweet old man and raised llamas for a living. The llamas were cool looking too, and reminded me of some old stuffed animals I used to pretend judged my karate moves (they always gave me 10/10). Jed's llamas, though, caused problems.

What was the problem with the llamas? Well, let's just say they weren't nearly as friendly as my stuffed animals. Anytime you tried to get close, they would spit. It wasn't normal spit either. It was a water cannon of spit and smelled horrible. We tried feeding them every once in a while, but it wasn't worth the risk. Why anyone would want to raise an animal like that baffled me.

Dad always asked us to throw the waste in the burn pile by the fence, but it was much more fun to catapult it toward the llamas and scare them if they were close.

I limped and dragged the poop shovel behind me all the way to the wire fence. Lumpy, one of the llamas Elliott and I had named because his tooth hung over his lip, was lying down eating some hay beyond the fence. He was well within my shooting range.

No one in sight, I grabbed the shovel and got into position. With the end of it behind me, I slid my hands up to the top grip, pulled back, and chucked the shovel forward as hard as I could. The poop left the shovel and sailed through the air in a giant cluster, spinning toward Lumpy.

He didn't see it coming, and it smashed him on the back of the neck. It's not what I meant to do, but it was kinda funny.

"Sorry about that, Lumpy!" I said, giggling. "Didn't mean to actually hit you like that!"

Lumpy stood up and whipped his head around. He looked right at me with his white tooth sticking out against his black fur coat. His neck was fully extended, which made him a good seven feet tall from head to toe. His black pool eyes narrowed, and he reared his head backward. Suddenly, Lumpy went into a dead sprint toward the fence. *He* was no longer the target; *I* was.

I wasn't stupid. I knew the small wire fence wouldn't stop him, and he could easily trample me into a pulp. I dropped the shovel and scooted as fast as I could across the pasture.

"Dad! Help!" I yelled.

The boot was slowing me down, and I couldn't find a rhythm with my feet. I kept looking back to see how much time I had left, but Lumpy was in full force, kicking up grass and mud as he galloped toward me. The thin wire fence was no match for Lumpy, and he busted through it without pausing and gained on me with each step he took.

I reached the backyard, but it was too late. Lumpy ran me over so easily it was like I didn't exist. His chest hit my back, and I fell to the grass while his hooves trampled over me. I grabbed my head for protection but not before the sound: **CRACK!** His hoof hit my boot, and I felt a familiar pain course through my body.

Nala came tearing around the corner, barking and yelp-ing, chasing Lumpy back into the pasture. Lumpy must have thought Nala was a vicious wolf, because he took off faster than he had run over me. Nala snipped at his heels until he was back on the other side of the fence. Then Nala stood guard at the fence and barked until Lumpy was almost out of sight. Her tail wagged back and forth with delight from the adventurous chase.

Mom, Dad, and Elliott had heard the noise and came rushing to my aid while I lay stunned in the grass.

"What happened?! Are you okay?" Dad yelled as he grabbed my shoulders and sat me up.

"I . . . ugh . . . the llama," I quivered.

Mom was already assessing the damage to my body. A small cut on my arm, a few scratches on my back, and a busted boot. Mom removed the straps from the boot and delicately, like a surgeon, pulled my foot out. Big Bubba didn't seem affected by the chaos and was the same size as yesterday, but the toe next to it was a little crooked and already swelling. It was broken for sure.

"Oh no! Now I know it's real! You're cursed!" Elliott said with exasperation.

The thought of him being right took the wind out of me, and I turned white. The dark feeling of nothingness came over me again, and I thought back to Eric and our conversation. The Curse. It was all adding up in my head. What kind of person could break two toes in a seventy-two-hour period? It couldn't just be a coincidence.

"Move, Elliott," Dad said. He threw me over his shoulder, brought me inside to the bathroom, and sat me on the toilet. Mom got some bandages and athletic tape from the cabinet and brought them in to start mending the toe. Dad knelt down; his dry, cracked hands held my foot up as Mom wrapped the gauze and tape around my newly broken toe. I winced and tried to yank my foot away, but Dad held strong and kept my foot in his hands. Big Bubba now had a friend taped to him. Two broken toes, together in a sleeping bag of tape—not how I pictured my summer turning out.

After I was taped up, I staggered to the living room couch with my foot raised on a pillow from my room.

"Here, take this," Mom said and handed me another handcrafted Deluxe Triple Scoop Caramel Blast. It tasted better than her last. She was getting good.

I ate my ice cream happily until Elliott showed up. He laid his head on the couch and had a giant smirk covering his face. "I told you: you're cursed!" he said and pointed at my biggest toe.

I flipped a wad of syrup in his hair, and he ran out of the room screaming. I was in no mood for his theory, but secretly, I was terrified. The dark feeling of nothingness was gone, but when I thought about it, my body remembered the cold.

Dad was on the phone talking to the doctor from Friday's visit, who told him to make sure my toe was taped to the other one. Check that off the list; we already did that. We didn't need to ask how long it would take to heal either; everyone knew it would be three to four weeks, the same as the others.

Later, when I washed up for bed, Dad fixed my boot. It wasn't completely destroyed, but it needed a few pieces of duct tape to keep the top together. I guess if it got worse, I could always throw on one of Elliott's busted rollerblades as a temporary solution.

The night ended much different from usual. Instead of Mom tucking us in like always, Dad did. He visited Elliott, then came into my room and looked me straight in the eye. His eyes said he was tired and worn out, but his face was full of seriousness. I expected a long lecture, so I sat up and leaned against my pillow for support when he started talking.

"Matt, sometimes life can get really tough, and it can throw some tricky curveballs that you don't see coming. You follow me?"

I nodded to show him I was listening.

"You can't let those curveballs bother you either. You have to tackle those problems, confront them head-on . . ." He paused and gently touched my shoulder. "And if you get beaten, you *never* take your frustrations out on your family." He was tearing up a little. "I shouldn't have yelled at you today. I'm sorry. I hope you can forgive me." With that, he leaned over, kissed my forehead, patted me on the shoulder, turned off the lights, and slowly shut the door.

I never did find out what had happened to Dad at work

that day, but I didn't need to, and I didn't care, because that was the moment I knew I wanted to grow up and be just like my dad—a person who was strong and caring and who could even admit when he was wrong. That's what I wanted to be. Dad knew how to handle *anything*.

I went to bed that night and dreamed of Lumpy. He trampled me on the soccer fields, the marketplace, and my house. Even in my dreams, I couldn't control that animal. Each time Lumpy tackled me, though, Dad was there to comfort me, and he said the same thing each time: "You can't let those curveballs bother you either. You have to tackle those problems, confront them head-on."

And guess what? Those words of advice Dad had spoken would help me get through the next seven broken toes too—I just didn't know it yet.

CHAPTER 9
WORK, WATCH, AND WAIT

Even with another broken toe in the boot, the next four weeks were the busiest of the summer. I was constantly on guard. After breaking another toe, I was starting to believe in the legend of the Curse. I mean, how else could you explain three broken toes in such a small amount of time? Breaking Jenna's collarbone had inexplicably resulted in cursing myself, and I didn't know how to break the spell. How many toes would I break? What else would break? An arm? A nose?! The unknowingness tortured me each time I thought about it.

I moved slowly wherever I went and jumped at any sudden noises. It was exhausting being on guard all the time. I never knew what to expect. Would I be attacked by Lumpy again? Trip over a hose? Would a falling piano land *smack* on another toe? Thoughts of the Curse drained me, and it didn't help that I was doing more activities than I'd ever done before.

Five days a week, from 8:00 a.m. until 12:30 p.m., Elliott and I worked at the Klinkles'. The work still sapped our energy with each rock we moved, but at least we started to make some visible progress. Instead of randomly picking up rocks, we developed a system. We started on the far-left corner of the yard and moved across the yard in patches. We'd mark off a section to focus on and wouldn't leave that spot until every single rock was gone from that area. When all we could see was dirt, we considered it done and gave the area a name.

Elliott would say something like, "Area Mudsville complete, sir!"

And I'd respond something like, "Check that! Moving on to next area!"

It seemed a little childish, but working the yard this way made us feel like we accomplished something, and it helped make the day go faster.

After moving stones all morning, I'd grab a quick lunch and carpool with Eric to soccer practice. Coach Cup wanted the team trained and ready by the Turkey Shoot-Out Soccer Tournament in October. I obviously couldn't play yet, but Dad said I should go watch.

"It'll be good for you, buddy. You know, show those guys you are still part of that team and . . ."

I zoned out while Dad said something about dedication or responsibility. All I could think about was how it would feel to sit there and not play.

"And maybe you'll learn a thing or two watching soccer instead of playing it. Matt? Matt? Pay attention. I'm trying to tell you something important," Dad said.

I snapped out of my dreaming. "Huh?"

Dad rolled his eyes. "I said you might learn a thing or two while you sit."

Turns out he was right. I actually *did* learn something— watching soccer is boring.

From 2:00 until 4:30 p.m., I watched Eric and the rest of my teammates pass the ball, shoot on the goal, and practice set plays to use during games. It was tough just sitting there, and I got all itchy watching everyone move freely around the field while I sat trapped in my boot. Stupid toes.

One day I got so antsy I grabbed a ball from the bag and took some shots with my left foot. I only got a few shots off before Coach Cup grabbed me by the ear and brought me to the sidelines.

"If you even think about getting on the field before you're completely healed, I'll make sure you sit on that bench forever!" Coach yelled loudly and plopped me on the steel bench.

The only time I didn't want to be on the field was from 4:00 to 4:30, when Coach Cup spent the end of practice yelling at everyone. On Wednesday, the yelling from Coach was especially brutal.

"You're a bunch of talentless grass weaklings! I could squeeze more talent out of a rat! You're all worthless!" he barked. He threw his clipboard down, picked it back up, and threw it down again. "How do you expect to win any games out there if you aren't any good?!"

It was the same speech as always, and even Coach Reese was getting tired of it. Eric didn't seem to mind, though. He just looked happy to be out there. We both knew, though, that as soon as I healed, his dream would be over. But he fought hard and was making some improvements with his shooting and passing. Coach Cup even noticed and complimented him one day. "Great shot, Eric! That's what we're looking for!" he applauded.

The entire team froze. This was a big deal. You have to understand that a compliment from Coach Cup was like winning the lottery—*twice*. It never happened. Eric about fell over when Coach said it, and Coach Reese twisted his finger in his ear to make sure what he heard was real.

So that was basically my schedule for four weeks: work,

watch, and wait. Work for four hours, watch soccer for two, and wait *forever* for my toes to heal.

Finally, after what seemed like the whole summer, I was able to take my foot out of the boot on August 2, leaving me with four weeks left of summer vacation before sixth grade. Big Bubba and his taped friend, which I had appropriately named Turd after what had happened with Lumpy the llama, were finally ready to take on the world again.

But with a month left in summer vacation, the Curse was just getting started.

CHAPTER 10
ERIC'S CURVEBALL

After a miserable four weeks in the boot, I could finally fulfill the dream of playing on the competitive soccer team. I hadn't touched a soccer ball in about a month (except when I got caught by Coach Cup for trying to shoot at the goal during practice), so I had some catching up to do. The rest of the team had had a month of training already, but I knew I could handle the pressure. As long as the Curse didn't strike again, I would be fine.

I decided not to tell Eric that I was healed and ready to play. How would I break the news to him that his time on the team was over? Would I pat him on the back and say, "Gee, thanks for covering for me, Eric; you can leave now"? No! It would crush him, and no words or actions of mine would help. Eric had put in a month of hard practice, and Coach Cup hadn't even scheduled a single game yet. His time on the field was over.

It was the first Monday in August, and instead of car-pooling with Eric, I rode my bike to practice so I wouldn't be forced to talk to him. Coach Cup would have to break the news to Eric himself. The ride through our town took longer than I thought, and I pulled up to the soccer fields a little late. The team was already in a circle near the middle of the field, stretching, with Coach Cup and Coach Reese at the sideline looking over some papers. I locked my bike up to the fence post and sprinted past the water fountains to my team. Man, it felt good to run again. I imagine it's how a dog feels when the leash is off—pure freedom.

I made sure to sit away from Eric, and I found a spot across the circle. I joined the team on some standing toe touches while my teammates welcomed me back.

"All right, Matt! Toes better?"

"You still got speed? We're gonna need it."

"Are you ready to play again? We have a scrimmage tomorrow!"

It felt nice to be wanted like that. As I answered their questions, Eric looked at me from the other side of the circle. His expression was blank, like someone had stolen all the feelings from his body—and it made me feel like garbage. He managed to wave, then he put his head back down toward his toes.

Life was throwing a curveball, like Dad had told me about when he'd tucked me in that one night. Only this curveball was meant for Eric. Eric had worked hard all summer to play on this soccer team, and now life was taking it from him. It wasn't fair. And it wasn't fair that Jenna had a broken collarbone. Because of me, two Monkling kids were miserable.

I took a deep breath and walked through the circle toward Eric. I didn't know what I was going to say, but I had to say something. As I thought about the possibilities, Eric cleared his throat and spoke up first.

"Hey, Matt, I wanted to say thanks."

I was confused. "Um, for what?" I asked.

"I know what you did. Coach Reese told me the first day of practice how you told him I should take your spot."

"But you only got to play for a month," I said. I had no idea where this conversation was heading, but at least he wasn't mad.

"Well, that's true, but I learned a lot, and I got a lot better too. Coach Cup says my shooting improved and that next year I could try out again and maybe make the team."

I still didn't know what to say, so I just stayed quiet.

Eric kept talking, though. "So, I guess, thanks for thinking I could do it. It meant a lot to me to play for the team, even if it was just for a little bit."

My tongue kept stumbling over the words. "Sure . . . I mean, yeah! You will definitely make the team next time!" It wasn't the best comfort I could give, but it was all I could think to say.

"Plus," Eric teased, "now I've got more time to practice karate moves and take you down!"

We both laughed, and I gave him a low high five. Eric was taking things well and handling them much better than I would have—that's for sure.

I glanced over to Coach Cup and Coach Reese, and they were in a loud argument. Whatever it was, Coach Cup wasn't happy about it, and he was high on his toes, yelling at Coach Reese. Coach Reese just stood there, arms across his chest and looking at Coach Cup like he was waiting for him to be done. He even sported a little smirk on his face as he adjusted his hat.

Coach Cup screamed one last "FINE!" in Coach Reese's face, threw the clipboard down, and stormed off toward the restrooms. Coach Reese picked it up and dusted it off, then jogged over to the center of our circle.

"Where is Coach Cup going?" asked one of our teammates loudly.

Coach Reese glanced back at the restrooms and chuckled. "Oh. Ha. He's just taking a little break from the heat. Don't worry about it. Anyway, I've got news!"

The team sat down to take a break while Coach Reese flipped some pages back on the clipboard.

"As you all know, Matt is back from his injury, and we are happy to have him—"

A cheer from the team erupted, and it gave me a proud, tingly feeling all over.

"But that means we will be losing one player who has worked with us all month," he continued.

My tingly feeling went away as quick as it had come. I still felt bad for Eric. I turned to look at his face. He was scratching his head, like I expected.

Coach raised his voice a notch. "Coach Cup and I were just speaking, though, and we decided—*together*—that it's not fair for someone to work hard and not get rewarded. That's why we've decided to add another spot to the roster and have Eric as a permanent member of our team."

A second cheer exploded, and I watched as the team ran over to Eric. I did not see that curveball coming. I thought Eric was getting kicked off the team for sure.

Eric's face was the brightest I'd seen it in months, and he shot me a quick thumbs-up right before the team swarmed him with high fives and pats on the shoulder. I looked back at Coach Reese to see his reaction, but he'd already moved on and started flipping through more pages on the clipboard.

The day couldn't have ended any better. Eric called his mom right away to tell her the good news and asked whether he could walk back home with me. I unchained my bike from the fence, and while we walked, we celebrated all the way home, bragging about all the goals we would score together that year.

It wasn't long before Eric brought up the Curse, though. "I've been meaning to ask you," Eric said hesitantly. "How do you feel about that whole Curse thing I told you about?"

I kicked some dirt off my front tire and chuckled. "To be honest, I don't know what to think. For a while, I thought you might be right, but . . ."

"But what?"

"Well, I haven't broken a toe in a while," I said. "I don't believe it. There is no Curse."

Eric stopped walking and grabbed my wrist. "Look, I know I'm not going to convince you right now, but you've gotta believe me, Matt. Be careful! The Curse is not to be messed with."

"Can we drop it and talk about soccer instead?" I interrupted. "I don't want to fight about it."

He shrugged his shoulders, and we went back to talking about soccer and the Turkey Shoot-Out Tournament.

But just like Eric's curveball, some things you don't see coming. And I learned that the hard way.

CHAPTER 11
MR. KLINKLE'S PAPER BAG

After three more weeks of hard labor in the Klinkles' backyard, Elliott and I were finally on our last day of work. It was the last week before summer officially ended, and Elliott and I, for the last time, filled up the wheelbarrow and hiked over to their backyard.

The walk to the Klinkles' went slower than ever before. Since my talk with Eric, I had felt uneasy. The dark nothingness feeling had returned shortly after our conversation, and for three weeks it had lingered on my shoulders. I couldn't shake it. It followed everywhere I went, and I found myself constantly looking for something bad to happen. I felt and looked miserable, and Elliott finally brought it up.

"Hey, Matt, why do you look like someone hit you with this?" he said and tried to pick up the sledgehammer from the wheelbarrow. "The past few weeks you've looked downright horrible!"

I chuckled while he struggled to hoist the hammer onto his shoulder. "I dunno. Just tired, I guess," I lied. "Why don't you put that thing down before you hurt yourself?"

"I can do it! Just watch me," he announced as he puffed his chest. He lifted the sledgehammer high into the air, and time suddenly slowed down.

The cold nothingness I had felt the past three weeks was now becoming more like a polar vortex in my nervous system, causing my back to tense and my mind to race. A hot sweat formed on my neck, and I could sense something bad was about to happen. Was it *the feeling?* Was it back?!

I watched as the sledgehammer slipped from Elliott's hands and began its descent back toward the ground directly toward my foot. Something was keeping my body from dodging it, and I could only watch as the hammer fell closer and closer to the ground. I winced and prepared myself for the pain.

"Move!" Elliott yelled and shoved me in the stomach, knocking me out of the way as the head of the sledgehammer went into the ground. It clanged against the pavement, creating a dent the size of my fist in the middle of the street.

"Why didn't you move?" Elliott asked. He put his hands on the sides of his head. "Are you *trying* to get hurt?!"

"You're the one w-w-who dropped the s-s-sledgehammer!" I stammered back. "I told you not to pick it up! You could have broken my toes!"

Elliott covered his mouth with both hands and took a few steps backward. "It's the Curse, Matt! Don't you see? It tried to get your toes again!"

I looked at the large hole in the street and then back at my foot. What else but the Curse could explain the cold nothingness feeling and three broken toes?

"You're welcome," Elliott boasted while he tried to pick up the sledgehammer. "I saved you from another broken toe."

I helped him pick up the hammer and put it back in the wheelbarrow. I was too shocked to admit to him that he might be right about the Curse, so I just muttered the only thing I could.

"Um, thanks, Elliott. I owe you one," I said and pushed the wheelbarrow up the Klinkles' driveway.

He started to say something back to me, but I ignored

him. All I could think about was the Curse. It was real, and I couldn't deny it any longer.

We each took out a shovel and stuck it in the dirt to lean on as we admired our work. A yard that had once resembled a gravel pit now looked more like a beach of black dirt, except for the occasional weed popping up here and there. It was a wonderful sight—no more rocks to move, which meant no more hurting backs. Our only job that last day was to pull the last standing weeds out of the ground. A piece of cake compared to moving rocks!

Elliott and I worked the small field as a team, picking areas and attacking them together to make work go faster. Elliott dug at top speed and kept chanting, "This is dumb . . . but we're almost done," in a steady beat as he slammed the shovel in the dirt.

I laughed and joined him to form a singing-brother digging team. We pulled weeds back and forth across the yard, chanting our song and smiling at the thought of actually being able to enjoy the last weekend of summer vacation without working at the Klinkles'.

At 11:37 a.m. on Tuesday morning (yes, I remember the time exactly), Elliott pulled the last weed out of the ground and threw it in the wheelbarrow. We were officially done, and we high-fived each other so hard it burned. Being done at the Klinkles' was a moment I'd never forget. I had no broken toes, I didn't have to move any rocks, and we would finally get paid money for all the work we'd done.

We hadn't seen Mr. Klinkle much since our first day on the job, but I remember he wanted us to knock when we were finished. I made Elliott come with me this time, and we walked to the back porch together. As we approached the steps to the screen door, Elliott pulled on my sleeve. "Hey, Matt, I've never seen Mrs. Klinkle—have you?"

It was a good question. "Hah! No, I guess I haven't. She's probably calculating how much taller Mr. Klinkle will get," I joked.

Elliott slapped my shoulder and laughed. "That's funny, Matt! Hey, speaking of, how much do you think we'll get paid, anyway?"

I'd been wondering the same thing. I was imagining it would be about $200 each, since it had taken almost two months and we'd worked fours days a week, but I rounded up to impress Elliott.

"Oh man, I bet it will be close to $300 each! Think of how long and hard we worked, Elliott! We'll get plenty of money, I'm sure."

Elliott's face lit up with excitement, and he pumped his fist back and forth while naming all the stuff he would buy. "I'm gonna buy a unicycle, a movie projector, a spaceman suit, marbles, a fire truck, a—"

"Yeah, yeah, Elliott," I interrupted. "I get it, I get it. Save your blabbing for later. Let's just get the money and get out of here."

Elliott nodded, and I knocked on the screen door. I heard rustling from inside the house and immediately felt the rumblings in my legs. Elliott grabbed my waist and looked around with a quivering lip as the porch continued to shake.

"Elliott, grow up," I smirked as I tried to pry him off. "It's just Mr. Klinkle walking. He's just super tall, remember? Like a basketball player."

I guess for Elliott's small body, Mr. Klinkle walking and shaking the porch was more like an earthquake, so I let him hold on to me and I straightened my stance for balance.

The rumbling slowly came to a stop, and the screen door opened to reveal Mr. Klinkle. He was exactly how I remembered him: dirty and tall. He coughed as he yanked the back of his jeans up to keep them from falling, and he used his other hand to scratch his hairy stomach. He stared at us a minute, squinting his eyes to take us in.

"Who are you?" he bellowed.

"Um . . . I'm Matt, and this is my brother, Elliott," I said. Was he kidding? How did he not know who we were?

His next sentence took awhile to get out. "Yeah, and"— pause—"what do"—pause—"you want?"

Did he really not know who we were? I tried again.

"We came to collect our pay, Mr. Klinkle. We've been working for you for almost two months, and we finished the job today."

Mr. Klinkle hiked up his pants again and raised an eyebrow. "Who? For what? Oh . . . take the brown"—pause—"paper sack on the front porch. It's got what you"—pause—"want."

With that, Mr. Klinkle took a step backward and shut the door. It made a gust of wind hit our face.

"Elliott, what do you think he meant by—" I turned around in time to catch Elliott sprinting around the house.

"Hey, wait for me!" I yelled. I jumped the stairs and sprinted around the side of the house with enough time to see a hand emerge from the front door and drop a small brown paper bag onto the front porch.

Elliott got to the bag just as the hand went back inside and shut the door. He tore open the top to see what was inside. "Yes, yes, yes!" Elliott shouted. "Money, money, money! Hooray!"

I looked over his shoulder into the bag. He was right—it was money—but it didn't look like much.

"Pour it out, Elliott. Let's see it," I said, anxious to get my hands on some cash.

He spilled the money onto the porch. Crumpled dollar bills, nickels, and pennies rolled onto the deck; Elliott scraped them up into a pile before they all got away. I unfolded the dollar bills while Elliott organized the change. Finally, when it was all organized, I counted it all up while Elliott sat and waited.

It didn't take long, and when I was done, I shook my

head. The number couldn't be right. I counted again. Same number.

Elliott was getting really curious and put his head over the pile of money. "How much, Matt? How much?"

"Elliott, just chill for a second, okay? I need to think."

Elliott frowned and sat back on his knees.

I counted one last time and got the same number. The total amount was sixty-two dollars and twenty-eight cents. We'd been robbed.

"Well?!" said Elliott. "How much?"

"We each get about thirty bucks," I moaned.

"What?! That's not fair! You've gotta say something, Matt! You have to! You have to!" Elliott pounded his feet on the deck.

"Fine, *okay*, Elliott. Calm down and take a seat. I'll take care of it." I was mad too, but I figured there must have been some mistake.

I knocked on the front door, but nothing happened. I didn't feel the deck shake like it had before. I knocked again, harder. Still nothing. I started to raise my fist again when the blinds of the window next to the door flew up. In the frame was the face of Mr. Klinkle.

"Who are you? What do you"—pause—"want?" asked Mr. Klinkle.

I tried to be polite. "It's Matt again, sir. I think you gave us the wrong amount of money. We worked all summer, not a week."

Mr. Klinkle coughed and waved his hand across his face. "Nope. That's the amount your sister and I agreed on last Christmas. No changes."

"What?!" I put my face close to the window and yelled, "What are you talking about?! I don't even have a sister!"

"That's that. We agreed." Mr. Klinkle smiled and waved. "Have a good"—pause—"day!" The blinds shut, and Mr. Klinkle disappeared.

My body shook with rage. "Wait! You can't do that!" I screamed. I ran over to the door and started bashing it with my foot to make him come out. "You didn't pay us enough!"

Elliott kicked the door too, with his stubby little legs. "Yeah! I have new toys to buy!"

We kicked the door over and over, but it never opened. We stepped back and looked at each other in disbelief.

"It's your fault, Matt!" Elliott whined. "Your Curse is bringing us bad luck everywhere!"

I got defensive fast. "Listen up, Elliott. I don't need you telling me something I already know, okay? Let's just see what Mom says about all this."

Elliott's mention of the Curse had brought me back to my reality. Before I could find a solution, though, I needed to focus on the Klinkles for now. I wanted my money, and the Curse was not going to stop me.

We gathered our shovels and ran back home to find Mom and Dad sitting on the back porch, sipping some tea.

"Boys! How'd it go? Did you finish today?" Mom asked.

"He only paid us thirty bucks each!" Elliott yelled. "You need to go talk to him!"

"Huh," Dad muttered while he took a swig of his tea. "That tracks."

"Wait, you knew about this and didn't tell us?!" I said, very shocked.

"We thought it would be good for you boys to do some volunteering this summer anyway. You should feel lucky you got paid at all!"

Elliott was already tearing up, and I was close to doing the same. We'd spent our whole summer over there, sweating our butts off, and we got paid hardly anything.

"Now, before you get emotional," Dad said, "your mom

and I want to thank you for working so hard this summer. It was wonderful you worked so hard for the Klinkles, so this winter we're going to buy you each a season pass to ski at Telluride. We can go whatever weekends you want during the winter."

A season pass? That was unbelievable! We usually went to Telluride only once a winter to ski. Working with the Klinkles had finally paid off, and the Curse, for now, was paused—all thanks to Elliott pushing me out of the way of the sledgehammer.

Elliott and I hugged both Mom and Dad as they winked at each other. Who knew that volunteering stuff could be so rewarding!

Mom added one last note. "Hey, how about I pitch the tent in the backyard, and you both can ask Eric and Kyle over for a camping sleepover?"

That night, the Monkling boys came over to celebrate the end of the summer. We grilled hotdogs, roasted marshmallows in the driveway firepit, and played cards in the tent until it got so dark you couldn't see your own hand.

At the end of the evening, we got in our sleeping bags, and Nala joined us in the tent as we snuggled in. She bounced around from boy to boy, trying to find the perfect spot to sit. She finally curled up next to me and let out a long breath of air. I felt the same way after a long summer and closed my eyes to remember all the things that had taken place in June, July, and August.

I rolled over, put my hand over Nala, and pulled her closer to my sleeping bag. A light pierced the tent and hit the lid of my eye, making everything seem red for just a second. I opened my eyes and glanced out the tent window at the Monklings' house. There sat Jenna under a lamp, both arms resting on the windowsill, looking down at our tent. She giggled, reached up, and clicked the light off, making the entire moment seem like a dream. She appeared much happier than the other times I'd seen her, and it was comforting, but I still wanted to talk to her.

I rolled over to my back and shut my eyes. What a summer! Jenna's broken collarbone, working at the Klinkles', the Curse that claimed three broken toes . . . it was overwhelming. At least I thought the Curse would be over soon. There was no way the Curse could get me in school.

Or at least that's what I thought.

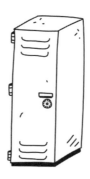

CHAPTER 12
THE DEAL WITH GRACE

The first day back to school is weird, isn't it? You can't decide whether you're really excited to go back or completely terrified. Here's how it usually plays out in my head the night before school starts:

Why Going Back to School Is Awesome:
1) Get to hang out with friends I haven't seen all summer.
2) Buy new clothes to impress everyone.
3) Play other sports on school teams.
4) Go on field trips.

Why Going Back to School Stinks:
5) Math is hard.
6) Some teachers are mean.
7) Homework.
8) Less free time in the day to do what I want.

9) Bullies.

10) Can't do karate at school.

11) Parent-teacher conferences.

12) Report cards.

13) Tests.

14) Pop quizzes.

15) More homework.

Even though the "Stinks" list is much longer, I was still looking forward to sixth grade. Sixth grade meant a lot of new things for me. For example, I would be in a new building instead of the small elementary school. Rather than Oak Grove Elementary, I would now be going to Centennial Middle School in the center of town, which held sixth, seventh, and eighth graders. I'd heard great things about it from kids on my soccer team, but some of the info I'd gotten sounded like the middle school would be much different from the elementary school.

For starters, Centennial mixed grades. The new classes (shop, climbing class, gym, and computer drawing) would have both sixth and seventh graders. Weird, but that meant I might be able to get a class with Eric, since he was going into seventh grade.

Each student got their own locker too. This was new to me, but I could handle it. Piece of cake. But I also heard each teacher assigned homework every day. *Not* a piece of cake—more like a piece of garbage.

Even so, I was ready to get out of the elementary school where fifth graders and kindergartners still had recess and lunch together. I needed a change, and on September 1, I got one. Life sent me a curveball.

On the morning of the first day of sixth grade, I had everything prepared. My clothes were laid out on the edge of my bed (gray sweatpants, my favorite hockey shirt, and red sneakers), and my green snowboarding backpack was filled with the supplies I'd need for my locker and classes. As soon as my alarm rang for me to get up, I bolted straight to the bathroom to take a shower and pushed Elliott over in the hallway on my way there.

I let the hot water hit the top of my head, but I could still hear Elliott pounding on the bathroom door from the hallway. "Hey! I was gonna take a shower, Matt! C'mon, get out!"

I ignored him, and while he yelled for Mom, I thought about all the possibilities for the day. Maybe woodshop would be first, then gym or even computer drawing. They all sounded so cool! Who would be my locker neighbor? Maybe Eric! That would be perfect! So many possibilities. I started listing them with soap on the side of the shower door, but Elliott had recruited Mom and brought her to the bathroom door before I finished.

"Matthew!" Mom said in her best motherly voice. "You

have exactly one minute to get out before I shut the water off to the entire house! Do you understand?"

"Whoa! Calm down, Mom. I'm working on it!" I yelled through the door. I skipped washing my hair and jumped out of the shower and smacked Elliott with my towel on the way out.

"Ow, Matt! Stop it!" Elliott complained and pushed me aside to squeeze into the bathroom.

I spent the rest of the morning sitting at the front step waiting for Mom and Elliott to get in the car. I was so pumped to leave and see the new school I couldn't stand it anymore!

Finally, after what seemed like forever, Mom got Elliott to the car and we were off. Oak Grove Elementary was just around the corner, so we dropped Elliott off first and wished him a happy first day of third grade. He kissed Mom and ran off toward Kyle, who was dancing around the flagpole near the front office. After Elliott left the car, I told Mom to step on it.

"Hurry or we're going to be late!" How embarrassing would it be to walk in late on the first day of school? I wasn't going to be *that* kid.

Mom didn't seem concerned at all, though. "Matt, we'll be fine. Do you have everything you need?"

"Yeah, I double-checked everything last night and this morning," I said while I tinkered with the window button.

"Are you sure, Matt? Did you grab the stuff off the kitchen counter—"

"Mom, I said I got everything, all right?! C'mon . . . get off my back!"

I'll admit it was a rude comment to make to Mom. She was only trying to help, and I could tell I'd hurt her feelings a little. The rest of the car ride was quiet until we pulled up to school.

Mom broke the awkward silence. "Bye, Matt. I hope you have a fantastic first day of school. I love you."

"Yep, bye," I said. And with that, I grabbed my backpack and shut the car door.

Before I ran off inside the school, a small siren went off inside my head that made me turn around to look at Mom, who was still staring at the steering wheel. I'd almost forgotten the most important part of the day—well, the most important for her, at least.

I ran to the driver's-side window and kissed her on the cheek. "Sorry, Mom. I love you too. See you later."

My kiss must have triggered something inside her, because she started crying right there in front of the school.

"Oh, Matt, you are growing up so fast! I feel like you were just in diapers yesterday," she sniffled through the waterfall of tears.

"Mom! Not now, okay?! Not in front of everyone," I pleaded. Getting dropped off late is embarrassing, but Mom crying in front of the school was potentially catastrophic. She needed to leave before anyone saw.

"Oh, I'm sorry!" she sniffed. "I'll get going." She pulled

herself together quickly and started driving away, waving. "Have a great day at school!"

I gave a quick flick of my hand to Mom and turned around to view my new school. Nothing out of the ordinary, just some brick walls, a couple windows, your typical middle school. Hopefully, it would be a place I'd rule by the time sixth grade was finished. With that final thought, I took a deep breath and opened the double doors to the main hallway.

I've never been to a real circus before, but I'll bet it looks a lot like the hallway of Centennial Middle School. I could barely see down the hallway! There were paper airplanes stuck to the ceiling, spilled energy drinks on the ground, kids climbing the drinking fountain . . . it was out of control. Some students were standing at their lockers listening to music, and some were already in groups roaming the halls, pointing and laughing at things as they walked by. I recognized a couple soccer players walking together, so I waved.

"Hey, guys, over here! It's Matt!" I tried to yell, but they strolled right past me like I was invisible. Stupid seventh graders. I forgot that once school starts, cliques begin.

I reached in my pocket and took out a small sheet of paper that had my locker number and combination on it. Locker 247, combination 12-12-43. Seemed easy enough to remember. I weaseled my way through the mass of kids and kept my eyes open for my locker.

I'd never been in a place with such a variety of smells. Sometimes I'd get a waft of perfume, which smelled okay, but then I'd walk past a group of kids who must've forgotten to put on their deodorant and my nose would hit a wall of rotten egg smell. Then I'd pass the bathrooms, and well, you know what that smells like.

The changing smells were too much for me, and I started to feel dizzy, so I pulled the neck of my shirt over my face and started power walking through the hall in search of my locker. I got toward the end, and the clutter of kids lessened, so I was able to walk freely in the middle of the hallway. I kept looking for locker numbers, but all the kids were filling their lockers with supplies, and it was hard to see anything but the backs of their hairy heads.

When I moved closer to get a better look, a small hand emerged from the crowd and grabbed my shirt, pulling me through the sea of kids. I was about to scream for help, but then the owner of the hand showed her face. It was Grace.

I knew Grace from Oak Grove Elementary School. Unfortunately, we'd shared the same teacher in fifth grade, and I'd sat next to her all year. You would think that someone with the name Grace would be polite, caring, and loving, but not *this* Grace. She's the exact opposite. Of course, teachers thought Grace was adorable and perfect, but most people didn't know that there were two sides to Grace: the kiss-up-to-the-teacher side and the bossy, mean, manipulative side. If you caught her in the wrong mood, you'd better watch out, because she could easily make your life miserable.

I looked at Grace, who was still holding the front of my shirt. If you'd never seen Grace before, you would think she was a third grader. I bet I could put her in a class of third graders and no one could even tell the difference! She was the shortest girl in fifth grade and was probably now the shortest girl in Centennial Middle School. She wore her blond hair in a tight ponytail and always wore some type of pink clothing. Today was no exception either. She was pink everywhere, from the pink ribbon in her hair to her pink shoes. Pink, pink, pink. It's not that pink is a bad color or anything. In fact, I like it. But I had never seen her wear *all* pink before.

"Well, hello, Matt! Nice to see you again," Grace said cheerfully. "Guess what? Your locker is right next to mine!" She seemed happy, which was good news for me. I didn't want to see the dark side of Grace on the first day of school. And how did she know where my locker was?!

I slowly removed her hand and brushed off my shirt. "Hm, uh, that's cool, I guess. Thanks for helping me out there, Grace. This hallway is … a lot."

"Oh, I wasn't trying to help." Her voice had unexpectedly switched from happy to harsh and serious. "I need to tell you something."

"Um . . . okay?" I could sense Grace's bossy side was coming out. I needed to leave soon before she unleashed all of it.

She grabbed the combination sheet out of my hand and started opening my locker. She kept talking at a fast pace. "Matt, middle school is different. You can't just have friends anymore. You have to *date* people. You have to get a boyfriend or girlfriend or some kind of partner. That's how middle school works."

This was new information to me. Dating? *Girlfriend?* Huh? No way.

"Um. What happens if you aren't dating someone?" I asked. I was actually curious, because Grace seemed really determined for some reason.

"You don't get invited to anything," Grace said. "And I mean *anything*. No parties, no hangouts . . . just you. All. By. Yourself." She opened my locker door and shoved her books in the top shelf and kept going. "So since we each need to date somebody, I decided that it's probably best for you to be my boyfriend and me to be your girlfriend." Her peppy voice was back now. She crossed her arms and stared at me, waiting for my response.

"Does that mean you like me or something?" I asked.

"What? No! Why would you think that?" Grace laughed.

"Because you *just* said we were going to be boyfriend and girlfriend. Like, just now."

"No, Matt! Ew! We just have to *look* like we're dating so we can get invited to all the cool stuff. That's why I'm putting my things in your locker. We have to fake it. Get it?"

I did get it. But I didn't know what would be worse: fake-dating Grace or not getting invited anywhere. After thinking hard for a second, I decided it was best to make a deal with Grace. It would help us both out.

"Okay, Grace. I'm in," I said and stuck out my hand. "It's a deal."

Grace slammed my locker door shut, shook my hand, then yanked my shirt down until I was eye level with her. My head was almost as low as my belly button.

"Good. If we are going to pull this off," Grace whispered, "you are going to need to do exactly what I say or else people will figure it out." Her bossy voice was back, and it was starting to get louder. "And I mean *exactly*."

She let go of my shirt and brushed it off for me. Her voice switched back to peppy. How on earth did she change moods so quickly? It was like someone was pressing a button on her. "Now, I expect you to carry my books for me later today—that's why I put them in your locker, okay?" Her mood was happy again. "I'll see you after fifth period, and don't be late—or else!" She grabbed her backpack off the floor and disappeared into the hallway.

I looked at my watch. It was 7:50 a.m. I had been in middle school for only ten minutes, and I already had a girlfriend. Well, a fake girlfriend. What else could happen on day one?

CHAPTER 13
A CURSED OUTCAST

Turns out a *lot* can go wrong on day one. All the teachers that day gave out homework, we had to run a mile in gym, and I was late to each class because I kept getting lost. Do I even need to mention Grace? She was in all of my classes, which stunk for two reasons. One, I had to carry her books everywhere and, two, she wouldn't stop trying to hold my hand.

Day one of middle school ended with walking Grace to her bus stop. She made me promise to wait for her outside the school the next day so that we'd look like a couple. Instead of just ending things there like a normal person, Grace started screaming at the top of her lungs to everyone on the bus. "Matt's my boyfriend! He loves me so much! He calls me all the time!"

I poked her in the side to get her attention. "Grace. Grace! Knock it off! You don't have to be so dramatic about all of this on day one!" I said.

The bus rolled away with Grace safely inside. I saw Mom inside our rusty maroon car, waving at me to get my attention from the parking lot. I waited for the next bus to pass, then darted between some cars and made my way to our vehicle. Mom popped the trunk open, and I tossed my backpack inside and sat next to Elliott in the back seat. Mom immediately began with her barrage of questions. "Who was that a girl you were with? How was class? Did you make any friends? Were you in class with Eric? What was the best part of your day?"

In a lot of ways, Mom and Elliott are the same. They get so excited over small moments, and they always ask a million questions before they're satisfied. I don't like answering every single question, but I guess it's nice having a family who cares. I mean, if it were the opposite, they wouldn't talk to me at all, and that would make life tough and boring for everyone.

I took a deep breath to relax, then spent the rest of the ride home answering every single question Mom had. One thing I made sure to do, though, was clarify that Grace was *not* my girlfriend. Mom and Elliott just giggled and smiled at each other, like they were sharing some sort of secret. It ticked me off.

"She's *not* my girlfriend! I'm serious!" I yelled.

"Okay, okay, honey. We got it," Mom said, but she was still smiling.

Grace must have mind control, because she somehow

made Mom and Elliott believe she was my girlfriend without even talking to her.

I went to bed that night with the idea that day two of school would be much better. Even if I had to break some rules, I was going to make sure I didn't relive day one again.

Little did I know middle school still had recess—sort of. On day two during lunch, all students were let outside for about thirty minutes of free time. Kids were screaming and running all over the place, jumping on each other, shooting basketballs, chasing rabbits . . . The teachers could barely keep up with everyone. It was a riot out there.

I didn't recognize a single kid, but I thought basketball might be a good way to make some new friends. I ran over to the court to see whether I could play.

"Hey! Need another player?" I asked the group of basketball players shooting hoops.

"Sure!" said a kid. "Then we can play with a full team."

Great! I thought. *That was easier than I expected.*

"Whoa. Just hold up a sec." Another boy emerged from behind the small group and narrowed his eyes to examine me. You're the kid with the Curse!"

How did he know that? Besides Eric and Elliott, I was the only one who knew. Plus, the Curse hadn't even done anything in a long time. Other people overheard the conversation, and the crowd was getting bigger around the court. Whispers surrounded me, and I couldn't keep up trying to hear them all.

"It's definitely him," the boy continued. "Sorry, man, you can't play with us. I don't want the Curse rubbing off on me!"

The crowd took a giant step back, making me feel even more alone. The basketball kids left, the onlookers scattered, and even some teachers who were watching went back inside the building. The Curse, real or not, was destroying my chances of making any new friends.

Instead of standing there feeling bad for myself, though, my eyes were drawn to the field of yellow just beyond the school fence. It was a dandelion field, and I knew instantly what would cheer me up: bee catching.

What is bee catching? Simple. You find a flower with

a bee on it, then grab the bee with your hand. It gets your blood racing, and it makes me feel like a daredevil. I don't like to brag, but I am a pretty good bee catcher, and it's more of a skill than most people think. It requires three things: courage, a strong hand, and lightning-fast speed. I happen to have all three, which makes me practically unbeatable. There are way less dangerous activities to do at recess, so unless you are, well, *me*, I wouldn't try this. Elliott tried to play with me once, but he wimped out the first time he got stung on the forehead. He wasn't willing to practice after that.

The field was perfect for getting my mind off the broken-toe curse. There were hundreds, maybe thousands, of dandelions, and I could see the bees hovering over the field. It was a gold mine, but I didn't feel right keeping it to myself. I turned around and looked for Eric, but he was still nowhere to be found. I hadn't seen him on day one, either, or at soccer practice that same night. Maybe he was sick.

I glanced and saw two kids sitting on a bench near the doorway. One was a kid with a cool pair of tight shorts, and the other was a kid named John I recognized from Oak Grove Elementary. He wore inch-thick glasses and snorted whenever he laughed. The glasses reminded me of my favorite anime character when he was off-duty from his superhero work. Both of the kids were just staring at the ground, kicking dirt with their feet.

Since kicking dirt didn't seem like much fun, and since

they probably hadn't heard about the Curse yet, I ran over to John and his friend and invited them to tag along.

"John? It's John, right?" I asked.

John picked his shoulders up and looked at me. "Uh-huh. And this is my friend Henry," he said as he pointed.

Henry picked his face up, smiled, and then went back to kicking dirt.

I was running out of time to catch bees, so I gave them a choice. "Well, I'm going under the fence to the dandelion field to catch some bees. You can either sit here and kick dirt for the rest of recess or come into the field with me. Follow me if you want to come."

John and Henry looked at each other. "Aren't you that kid with the broken-toe curse?" asked John.

They both shook their heads, then started drawing circles in the dirt with their fingers. Whatever. The Curse had taken my friends away for the day, but I could still cheer myself up. I turned and sprinted past the green jungle gym, across the football field, and to the fence. The closer I got to the field, the stronger the smell of flowers got, and I could even hear the buzzing sound of the bees. The Curse would not control this moment. Not today.

The chain-link fence was too flimsy to climb, but I tried anyway. I got halfway up before it bent backward toward the ground, then shot straight back up when I let go. The only way to get to the other side was to go under. I dug my hands under the fence and pulled as hard as I could, but the bottom of the fence came up only a few inches. Even if I was greased with butter, I wouldn't be able to fit through.

I decided to try one last time to lift the fence. As I bent down to fasten my grip, four more hands reached down from behind me and started pulling: Henry and John. "Pull!" I screamed.

John and Henry arched their backs and pulled with everything they had. The fence lifted, and I scrambled underneath the fence and flipped on my back to the dirt. I jammed my feet up into the fence to hold it up while John and Henry squeezed their way under. John was a snake and got through easily, but Henry had a harder time. I swore I heard a **POP!** sound when the fence shot him out to the other side.

Henry brushed off his button-up plaid shirt, and John adjusted his glasses.

"What made you two decide to come?" I asked.

Henry spoke for the first time, in a voice higher than I'd expected from a kid his size. "I'll take my chances with the Curse. And John didn't want to be left alone," he muttered.

"Fair enough," I said. "Well, let's get started!"

I explained the game to them in about twenty seconds as the bees flew circles around our ankles. I expected both of them to chicken out and leave, but John was already trying to grab bees, and Henry wasn't far behind, so I let them practice for a few minutes while I took in the scenery. It was the largest bee field I had ever seen. I could look in any direction, and all I could see were bees and flowers. I could tell I was going to spend a lot of lunch recesses on this side of the fence.

I got on my hands and knees and crawled through the field. I found a bee gathering pollen from a flower, his back turned toward me. Slowly, I got the clear plastic zippy bag from my pocket (and, yes, I do carry one around all the time—just in case). I raised my hand and brought it down so fast the bee stood no chance. **SNAG!** I removed my hand from the flower and picked up my first bee, placed him in the zippy bag, and continued on my quest. There were so many bees that at one point, I lost count of how many were buzzing in the clear bag.

I heard the bell ring in the distance, and John and Henry picked their heads up from across the field. We darted back to the fence and helped each other underneath, and as we walked together, we shared our bee-snatching stories.

"Matt, how many bees did you get?" Henry questioned as he emptied his pockets. "I only got a few and then let them go . . ."

"Same here," John added. "I think I got three or four."

"I'm not sure, Henry," I said. "I lost count."

I held up the vibrating bag. It was too hard to see, but it looked like a new record! Maybe twenty? I would have to get it home somehow to show Elliott, or he would never believe me. I let a little bit of air out of the bag and carefully put the buzzing bag into my front pocket. Henry looked at me curiously.

"It's okay." I assured him. "I've done this before. They're very safe."

We walked back inside, and as I left for class, I told them to meet me by the fence the next day. At least those were two people who weren't afraid to hang out with a boy with a broken-toe curse.

I walked into science class and took my seat next to a kid named Bobby. I was supposed to sit next to Grace each day (like she told me to), but I was doing my best to avoid her.

Grace slipped through the doorway just as I finished my thought and sat down behind me. "Why didn't you save me a seat?!" a devilish voice whispered in my ear. "Start acting more like a boyfriend."

"Maybe *you* should just relax," I said.

"Did you just tell me to relax?" Grace shot back. "Oh, you are gonna pay for that!"

Man, I was sick of Grace. As small as she was, she could really be intimidating. I tried to ignore her voice and got my books ready for class.

Mr. Latick, our science teacher, stood up from his desk and began the lesson like he had on day one: with a question. He cleared his throat and began. "Today we will be learning about matter and elements. Does anyone have any idea what the difference between the two is?"

I didn't know, so I put my hands in my pocket and felt the bees walking around their zippy home. Ugh! There was no way I could focus with all the vibrating happening in my pants. I had to move them before I got caught. I grabbed my backpack, opened the small front zipper, and tried to move the bee bag out of my pocket and into the pouch while some kid attempted to answer Mr. Latick's question.

Before I even got close to moving the bees in the backpack, Grace blurted out from her seat, "Mr. Latick! Mr. Latick! Matt is playing with something in his pocket, and it is distracting me from listening to you!"

I turned around to Grace, and she just smiled—the type of smile you make when you've done something sinister.

"Grace, don't," I whispered.

"Matt, will you please empty your pockets onto the desk so we can continue without any disruptions?" Mr. Latick demanded.

I wasn't going to let Grace win this one, not on the

second day of school. "Sorry, Mr. Latick. I'll empty them right now," I said.

I turned around and threw the bag of bees onto Grace's desk. She let out a high-pitched scream as the bee bag tumbled out of my pocket and buzzed across her desk. She pushed her chair back and ran out of the room as the kids pointed and laughed. I couldn't tell whether they were laughing at her or me, but I didn't care. I had given Grace a taste of her own medicine.

"Matt?! Are those . . . bees? That is unacceptable. Pick that up and consider this your warning for the year. One more stunt like that and I'll send you straight to the office, understood?! Now let them out the window!" Mr. Latick's voice was cold and stern, but he seemed distracted by Grace's absence from the class, and he left the room to find her without saying anything more to me.

I looked down at the desk and noticed something. It was the most bees I'd ever seen in my years of bee catching. I counted them up as I released them through the window. Forty-five bees. It was a new record, and I'd have to share it with John and Henry the next day. I sat back down in my seat as Mr. Latick walked in. He took one last look at me before he continued his lesson.

I got through class without falling asleep, and that concluded day two. I didn't have to take the bus home, because our competitive soccer team had its first soccer game at a nearby high school. Since I hadn't seen Eric all week, I didn't wait for him and walked by myself. By the time I got to the field, Coach Cup and Coach Reese were setting up the nets and water jugs for the game. I let them work while I joined the rest of the team. We put on all our gear and started the warm-up, and I asked whether anyone had seen Eric. No one knew where he was and said they hadn't seen him since last week. Hopefully, he would show up for the game.

Coach Reese and Coach Cup came over and gathered us into a circle to stretch. Coach Reese was quieter than usual, but Coach Cup was already at his peak level. He was yelling, throwing his clipboard, and making all sorts of commands. The game hadn't even started yet.

His speech didn't pay off in the end. I'll spare you the details of the game, but here are the highlights:

1) Eric never showed up.
2) We lost 4–1 to a team called Eagle Crest.
3) I got a huge cut on my knee from sliding on the grass.
4) Grace showed up to watch me play and said if I didn't go to the pool with her next week, people would probably find out we were faking our relationship, especially after what had happened in science class. She said it was "super important" we go on a "date."

Besides Grace showing up and telling me about our date, the day wasn't all bad. I got to spend thirty minutes with two new friends, catch bees, and make Grace think twice about embarrassing me in class. Also, I got in a lot of running that day. It's a good thing I did so much running too, because the Curse was plotting its next move, and running wouldn't be so easy for a while.

CHAPTER 14
TOES FOUR AND FIVE

After a week and a half in school, I finally felt like I was in a good routine. I knew all my teachers, had memorized my locker combination, knew the fastest route from one class to the other, and had even gotten an A on my first science test. Henry and John were in a couple of my classes too, and we spent every recess together, going under the fence to look for bees. The Curse, for the time being, had disappeared. But my label hadn't.

When I walked down the hall each day, I was reminded by classmates.

"Watch out, everyone! Don't let Matt the Cursed Kid touch you!"

"Hey, Cursed Kid! Maybe you should live in a plastic bubble so nothing can get you!"

"The Cursed Kid is here! Everyone, clear a path!"

I wasn't making any new friends, but at least Eric was

finally back in school. We were lucky enough to have one class together: woodshop. He walked in a little late but sat down next to me.

"Where have you been? I was starting to wonder whether your parents locked you up!" I joked, but Eric did not laugh.

He put his books underneath his desk and slowly turned toward me. His face was pale and drained of all energy. "I had the flu," he sniffled, then wiped some escaping boogers from his nose. "I couldn't even get out of bed without throwing up."

I backed up a little. "Oh man, that's really horrible. I'm sorry, man."

"Well, at least I don't have the Curse," he said firmly. "Hey, why didn't you call me to see where I was?"

"Um, I dunno," I shrugged. "I guess my brain was busy with the start of school and all. But why didn't you call me?"

Eric reached for a tissue from his pocket. "Because I heard the Curse is contagious, even over the phone," he smirked, then blew his nose. "I'd rather have the flu every day of the week than have that stupid Curse."

With that comment, Eric seemed back to his normal self. Later on that week, though, I invited him to hang out with John, Henry, and me, but he refused. He was talking with some of his seventh-grade friends when I asked, but then he just laughed and ignored me. The next day I asked him again and got the same response, except this time the entire group laughed. I tried to put it out of my mind, but

I didn't understand what Eric was doing. Whatever the reason, at least I had John and Henry to keep me company. Otherwise, I would have no one.

Soccer was about the same too. We'd won a weekend game shortly after our 4–1 loss to Eagle Crest, but Coach Cup wasn't happy with the win. He made us run the next practice for not "trying our very best" and not "acting like real soccer players"—whatever that meant. Coach Reese was having a hard time lifting the team's spirits like he usually did. Instead, we just got the lectures and yelling from Coach Cup *and* Coach Reese. Since the Turkey Shoot-Out Soccer Tournament was approaching, both coaches were trying their best to get us prepared. If we won, the team would get to travel to Las Vegas for an international tournament the following summer. It was a lot of pressure, but I'd never been to Las Vegas, so I was ready for any training that could get us there.

Life seemed to be going well, but my routine was quickly shattered by Grace one afternoon during science class.

"Pssstt! PSSSTTT! Matt! Turn around!" Grace grumbled. She was trying her best to whisper, but she sounded more like a broken steam engine.

"What do you want, Grace? Make it quick," I demanded. I'd been trying my best to make all our conversations short, but it usually didn't work.

"I just want to remind you that today we are going to the pool for our first date. Did you get me a present?" Grace said.

I was flabbergasted. "Huh? No, Grace, I did not get you a present. Are you serious? Why would I get you a present?"

"Because it's our two-week anniversary, silly!" she squeaked and giggled.

By now, everyone in class was watching, including Mr. Latick, so I had to end the conversation before it got any louder. I acted like I was writing to distract the teacher and made Grace a deal.

"Fine," I muttered. "I'll go to the pool with you today, but I am still *not* getting you a stupid present."

She ignored half of what I said. "Great! We'll walk together after school to the pool, and then you'll pay for me to get in!"

"Huh? Wait. What did you say? I am *not* going to pay for—"

I was interrupted by Mr. Latick clearing his throat and tapping the pencil on his desk. I'd already made a bad impression with Mr. Latick on the second day of school, so I just kept my mouth shut to avoid another lecture. Meanwhile, Grace started muttering a song she'd made up. She sang it the rest of the period. "Our first date, our first date, our first date will be so great! Our first date, our first date . . ." I had to admit, she was pretty good at acting this whole thing out.

Grace's song was stuck in my head for the rest of school. And at the end of my last class, just when I thought it was gone, I walked in the hallway and Grace appeared out of nowhere, singing her tune. The song was like a merry-go-round in my head, and it was driving me nuts. As we walked outside toward the bike path to the pool, Grace kept singing, trying to hold my hand, but she stopped when John and Henry waved and approached us.

"Um . . . excuse me!" Grace's grumpy and bossy voice switched on. "We are on our first date, and we have no time to talk with anyone."

John hid behind Henry, who said, "Oh! But . . . Matt invited us to the pool too!"

Grace's eyes widened, and she looked at me with disbelief. Ha! Grace might have her ways of manipulating people, but I had plans of my own too. After Grace had talked to me in science class that day, I'd grabbed John and Henry and asked whether they would come to the pool. That way, I wouldn't have to suffer with Grace all alone. She hadn't seen it coming, and there was nothing she could do about it.

"Ugh. *Fine!*" Grace rolled her eyes at the boys. "But you have to walk behind us on the way there."

The walk down the bike path seemed to go faster knowing John and Henry were behind us. I kept my hands in my pockets to avoid Grace, but she wrapped her arms around my waist as we strolled downtown past the post office, the grocery store, the flower shop, and the theater. Each time someone walked past us, Grace would raise her voice and boast, "Isn't it great that we're together? It's so perfect!"

I decided it was time I pitched in and at least tried a little bit. "Yes. Boy, does it feel good to be in a relationship!" It sounded so weird coming out of my mouth—it felt like a different language.

The looks we got from adults passing by were odd, like they felt sorry for us, so I kept my head down and tuned her out until we got to the pool.

The Montrose Pool was pretty big for a small town. It had an indoor pool with a couple diving boards and a hot tub, an outside pool with water games, and a giant water-slide where most of the kids hung out. That's where I planned on spending most of my time: riding the slide.

And just like someone would snap a finger, I found my eyes were transfixed on the slide as *the feeling* came over me.

It moved from my stomach to the tips of my shoulders, and the eerie sensation made me shudder. I looked around in all directions to see whether there was any danger. Last time *the feeling* had happened, the Curse had almost broken my toe with a sledgehammer. I continued to stare at the slide, waiting for something to happen, but it never did. The cold nothingness left me as quick as it had come, and I could only stare at the slide in shock.

Grace caught me gazing at it as we made our way to the front desk. "Snap out of it, Matt," she beckoned. "Where's the money for our tickets?"

I reached into my back pocket and pulled out seven bucks, which was only enough for one pass to the pool. I gave it to the clerk, who handed me a ticket and a towel.

"Um . . . Matt. Aren't you forgetting something?" Grace asked as she put her hand out in front of my face. She tapped her foot while motioning with her hand.

This was my chance to ditch Grace and actually enjoy the pool with just my friends.

"Nope!" I said and slapped her hand with a low high five. "See you later!" I took the towel and ticket and ran into the men's locker room. It was perfect! I didn't have extra money, and Grace had none! It would be just John, Henry, and me in the pool, and Grace would be stuck outside. I couldn't believe I hadn't thought of the plan earlier.

I found a locker and started jamming my shirt, shoes, and backpack inside. I was still laughing at the thought of

Grace standing in front of the desk, her jaw hanging open from shock.

Henry walked in with John close behind him. "What's so funny?" John asked.

"Oh man! Did you guys see that? She is going to be so mad. Did she scream? Ha! I bet she did. I don't even care! Now it's just the three of us!" I cheered with pleasure. I broke into my own version of Grace's song while I danced and sang, "Our first date, our first date! Too bad Grace is stuck outside!" It didn't rhyme, but it still made me laugh hysterically.

Henry and John weren't laughing, though. They frowned and looked at each other, then at the ground. They looked very suspicious.

I quit dancing and glanced at Henry, who was fiddling with the front of his shirt, and John, who was biting his lip. "Guys . . . what's up? Isn't this great?!" I asked.

John tried to explain. "Well . . . you see, you left so fast . . . and then the clerk looked at Grace, and she was screaming at you, and people were staring, and she was crying, and she didn't have any money, but we did . . ."

"You didn't," I said, my face blank. "Please tell me you didn't do what I think you did."

"We didn't know what to do, Matt! She was so angry! We just gave her some!" Henry bellowed.

"Come on, guys! You can't be serious. Did you really pay for her to get in?"

They didn't respond, which was an answer in itself. John and Henry, controlled by Grace's screaming and crying, had paid for her to get in. My ultracool spur-of-the-moment plan had failed, and Grace was probably already inside the pool waiting for me to get in.

"You gotta be kidding me," was all I could muster up.

I slowly shut the locker door and sat down on the dressing bench. I couldn't be too mad at John and Henry, since they'd agreed to come to the pool in the first place, but they'd still messed everything up, and they knew it. John was still staring at the ground, and Henry was swaying back and forth with his hands in his pockets. I couldn't afford to lose them now, so I just encouraged them.

"Don't worry about it, guys. You tried. Just get ready, and let's go to the slide."

The three of us walked outside to the pool together, all knowing that we had spoiled the chance of having a day without Grace, but the view of the slide made the feeling go away instantly. It was a beautiful sight. The slide seemed bigger, being so close to it now. It was three stories tall, and the white beams of the slide curled around each other like a coiled snake. I watched as kids shot out the bottom and plunged in the water, then immediately swam out to get back in line.

A voice broke my trance. "Over here, guys! Over here!" It was Grace, and she was already in the pool, waving at us with her nose plug on and a pair of large yellow goggles. I threw my towel aside and cannonballed into the water. The immediate rush of cold felt great as I sank to the bottom.

My rear hit the bottom of the pool, and I opened my eyes to see legs all around me. I swam toward the edge of the pool and splashed upward to find John and Henry. John was already in the pool swimming toward the deep end, but Henry was sitting with his button-up shirt on at the side of the pool with his feet in the water. He tugged his shirt down toward his shorts while I yelled at him.

"Hurry up, Henry! Get in before you fry out there!"

I could almost hear the gears in Henry's brain turning,

trying to make a decision. I could tell he wanted to get in, but he kept messing with his shirt.

I motioned for Henry to jump in, and that's when Grace appeared. I couldn't make out what she was saying, because she was whispering in Henry's ear. Before I could say or do anything, she and Henry grabbed hands and took a running start before jumping into the pool. He belly-flopped onto the water, and a giant **FLAP!** echoed across the concrete walls surrounding the pool.

"Haha! Did you guys see that splash?! It was huge!" And with that, Henry climbed out of the water, took off his soaking wet button-up shirt, and jumped in again, sending a small wave across the pool.

I hadn't expected that type of reaction from him at all.

Grace followed his lead and tried making a wave, but she barely made a splash, and we all laughed when she asked whether her jump was bigger than Henry's. John joined us and kept trying different moves to make a bigger wave in the pool. I looked over at Grace, who was now screaming directions at Henry on how to position his body to make the biggest splash-wave possible. She thought it was the coolest thing ever.

"You melon head! Get your knees up and tuck your arms in!" She glanced over and gave me a wink right before Henry made his biggest splash of the day.

I swam quickly over to Grace before Henry reappeared.

"What did you say to Henry?" I asked. "I thought he would never get in."

"I just told him I'd jump with him, that's all," Grace said, looking confused.

"That's it?!" I replied, baffled. "But I was motioning for him to come in the entire time."

"Well," Grace shrugged. "Sometimes you just need a friend next to you, right?" She winked, and then swam to the pool edge to join Henry for another jump.

Grace was annoying, bossy, and sometimes flat-out evil, but that afternoon I saw a different side of her. If it hadn't been for Grace, I bet Henry would still be sitting at the edge of that pool thinking about what to do, and I think Grace noticed that. Maybe she wasn't so evil after all. And maybe I could learn a thing or two from her too.

I joined in the splashing competition for a while, even holding hands with Grace once to jump in, but only *once*. It must have made her day too, because she wouldn't stop blushing and giggling for the next five minutes.

I, on the other hand, turned my attention to the slide. The line was finally short, so I ditched John, Henry, and Grace to get in before it got any longer. I jogged up the concrete stairs as water droplets hit me from the top of the tower. When I reached the final platform, the tan lifeguard was measuring a little kid's height to see whether he was tall enough to go down.

"Come on! Pretty please? I'm tall enough! Look!" the boy begged. He stretched his neck and stood on his toes. It was obvious to anyone that there was no way the kid was tall enough, but the lifeguard decided to let him go anyway. I blame him for what happened next.

The little boy grabbed the railing and, on the lifeguard's whistle, sat down and slowly scooted down the white piping. In all my life, I'd never seen anyone go so slow on a waterslide. It was almost like the boy was *trying* to go slow; he even had his arms out, touching the edge to keep himself from going fast!

"Hey, twerp!" I yelled from the balcony. "Get going, will ya? You're wasting everyone's time!"

He finally disappeared into the darkness, and I got ready for my turn on the tubed slide. On the lifeguard's whistle, I grabbed the bar and launched myself on the water and shot down the slide. I arched my back to gain top speed as I zipped around the bends of the slide like those athletes in sleds during the Winter Olympics. Water sloshed back and forth as I hit the turns, and my hair was beginning to feel dry because I was going so fast. Being in the dark made it seem like I was rocketing through space at warp speed, and I almost forgot the water was right beneath me.

I got closer to the end and heard echoes of laughter bounce throughout the tube, but they weren't coming from me. I rounded the final turn and picked up my head to prepare my body to hit the water. What lay ahead, however, was something I didn't expect. The little boy, the slowest water slide rider on earth, was climbing up the slide toward me.

I sat up and scrambled to stop myself, but my hands

only glided over the slide walls as I got closer. In a last-ditch effort to stop myself before colliding with the boy and mangling his small body, I kicked my feet to the ceiling of the tube and jammed myself in the slide.

It was the worst decision ever.

My body jolted stiff as I felt my left foot freeze up in pain, and my head smacked the slide with such force that it knocked me out cold.

According to John, my lifeless-looking body slithered out of the slide and plopped into the water like a bunch of seaweed sliding over a waterfall. The little boy, who wasn't hurt at all, came out riding on top of me. In fact, I guess he laughed and yelled "Again! Again!" while he jumped out of the pool and got back in line like nothing had happened. The little twerp didn't even care what he'd done!

Grace, who must be a lot stronger than she looks, helped a lifeguard pull me out of the water and onto the concrete. The sizzling-hot ground shocked me awake, and I woke up to the lifeguard, Grace, Henry, and John looking down at me as if I were a dead fish.

"Oh, Matt! Are you okay?! What happened?" Grace said as she held my hand.

I didn't have energy to fight her off this time, but at least she seemed genuinely concerned.

"I tried, um, to stop, um, myself, um, in the slide," I said.

"You shouldn't be playing around in the slide like that," lectured the lifeguard. He waved his finger at me and continued. "You could've seriously hurt someone!"

Were all lifeguards at this pool useless? This lifeguard thought *I* had been messing around, and the other lifeguard let a kid, who was too young and short, ride the slide.

Grace must have been thinking the same thing as me, because she looked at the lifeguard and said, "Why don't you do something useful and get him a bandage for his toes? Move it!" At least Grace was there to be bossy for me.

The lifeguard looked over at Grace like he was ready to lecture her too, but instead he stood up and walked away toward the building.

Wait. What had Grace said about my toes? I looked

down at my left foot and saw an all-too-familiar sight: my pinky toe and the one next to it were swelling, and the pinky toe was bleeding out the top a little bit. I tried to wiggle them to see what the damage was, but I couldn't.

Oh, and the pain? I'd rather not talk about it. Let's just say there were a lot of tears . . . and maybe a few screams.

Both toes were definitely broken. The Curse had stuck again, and the cold nothingness came back around me, sending goose bumps up my arms and around my back.

After the lifeguard wrapped my toes, John and Henry helped me hobble to the front desk, where I called Mom and told her what had happened. She said Dad had just picked up Elliott from piano practice and that he'd pick me up next.

John and Henry were a little stunned. "Um. I don't really know what to do for you, Matt," Henry said. "I think we'll leave," he continued, and they started their walk home.

"I'll stay with you," Grace said and sat next to me in the grass by the pool entrance. Neither of us said anything, but at that point, sitting next to Grace was better than sitting alone, and she stayed there until Dad pulled up ten minutes later. In that moment, it actually *felt* like I had a girlfriend. And I didn't hate it either.

Before Dad got out of the truck to help me in, Grace said, "I'll see you tomorrow, Matt. I can carry your books if you want help."

"Maybe. Thanks for staying."

Grace flipped her wet hair back and nodded. She

wrapped her towel around her waist and walked back inside, taking one last look at me before turning away into the locker room.

Dad helped me get to the back seat, and Elliott watched as I propped my foot up next to his armrest. As Dad walked around the front of the truck, Elliott couldn't contain himself. "Are they broken?" he asked.

"Probably," I said. "They feel broken anyways."

"The Curse!" he exclaimed.

"Shut it, Elliott."

"You can't deny it," he lectured. "How else can you explain all your broken toes?"

"Well, then, Mr. Genius, since you know everything, when will the Curse end?" I scorned.

"When all your toes break, I guess," Elliott stated in a matter-of-fact sort of voice.

I swallowed hard. Was he right? Is that what it would really take for the Curse to go away? Whatever. The Curse was a legend. He didn't know any better—he was only in third grade—but his statement made me nervous that I might have five more broken toes to go before the torture was over.

Dad got in the truck and asked a few questions about what had happened at the pool. I told him everything I could remember, then he made his assessment. "Looks like you did everything that you could do to stop from hitting that kid. Good job, Matt. That was quite the curveball life threw at you today, huh?"

"Yeah," I replied. But I wasn't sure what I was going to do. Soccer was coming up soon, and the Curse had reared its head again.

What else was it going to take from me?

CHAPTER 15
KARATE CARD

When Elliott, Dad, and I got home, Mom had already prepared a Deluxe Triple Scoop Caramel Blast, ready for me on the table. She kissed me on the cheek as I picked it up, and I smiled to let her know I appreciated it. I took the bowl to my room and spent the rest of the night in my bed with my foot on some pillows. I had some serious thinking to do.

The Curse was beginning to feel more real by the day, and I decided it was best to just accept it. I, Matt Sprouts, was cursed, and there was nothing I could do about it. There was no one to turn to, no one to ask advice from. It was just me and the Curse. Not exactly a comforting feeling, I can tell you that!

While I wondered how I was going to get rid of the Curse, Henry and John both called that night to see how I was doing. They were turning out to be pretty cool friends, not something I had expected after the first day I'd asked them to catch bees. After I ended the call with Henry, I called Eric to tell him about my day, but he didn't answer his phone—Jenna did.

"Hi, Matt," she said in the flattest voice ever.

"Um . . . is this Jenna?" I asked, although I already knew what the answer would be.

"Yes."

"Oh. It's Matt next door."

"I know. I saw your name pop up on Eric's phone."

There was a long, awkward silence.

I was about to hang up, but Jenna's voice cut the dead air. "Well, Eric isn't here, if that's who you're looking for," she said with a hint of disappointment. "He's in the bathroom."

"Okay . . . um . . . could you just tell him I hurt my foot and to call me back when he gets a chance?" I asked.

"Yeah. I can do that," she mumbled, and then it was silent. Our conversation was over.

Talking with Jenna had gone a lot better than I thought it would. I'd expected a screaming match between the two of us, but she didn't sound very mad at all, just a little disappointed for some reason. Part of me wanted to call her back, but I couldn't do it. Instead, I pushed the phone aside and shut my eyes, pondering how in the world I was going to play soccer with two broken toes.

I spent the night tossing and turning. It was one of those nights where everything goes wrong. My pillow seemed hot, the sheets were heavy, and every creak in the house kept my eyes open and my mind wandering. I tried every remedy I could think of to sleep. From 11:00 p.m. to 12:00 a.m., I read in bed. At 2:30 a.m., I went to the kitchen and made a snack. At 3:14 a.m., I moved to the living room couch to try to fall asleep. At 4:00 a.m., I got up from the couch and moved back to my room. Nothing worked.

When my alarm went off at 7:30 a.m. for school, not one part of my body felt ready, especially my toes. I didn't even bother to take a shower or eat breakfast. Instead, I got dressed in my gray sweatpants and T-shirt; put on my duct-taped, half-broken toe boot; and dragged myself into the front seat of the car. I counted dead flies on the window while I waited for Mom and Elliott.

When Mom got into the car, she interpreted my tired-ness as sadness. I bet she thought I was bummed about my broken toes, which I was, but she had no idea how tired I actually felt. She did her best to cheer me up, though, even telling an embarrassing story about herself that I'd never heard before. It made me chuckle, but that was all the energy I could give. My body wanted to shut down and curl into a tight ball.

We dropped Elliott off at school first. He couldn't help getting one last laugh as me as he got out of the car and pointed at my boot, but Mom stopped him immediately.

She called him back over to the car. "Elliott, would you like it if someone laughed at *you* if you were hurt?"

Elliott put his head down and shuffled his feet.

"Well?" Mom prodded.

"No," Elliott mumbled. "I wouldn't."

Mom turned around to include me in the conversation. "Whenever we get the chance, we should lift others up, right, boys?"

We both nodded.

"Sorry, Matt," Elliott mumbled again, sounding apologetic. "I'll see you later today."

He took off running before I could say anything back. I understood why though. Apologizing can be uncomfortable sometimes, especially when you realize how big of a mistake you actually made.

It wasn't long before we pulled up to Centennial Middle School. Grace was waiting by the front of the building. Mom reacted to Grace's presence just like I thought she would. "Ohhh . . . how cute! Your girlfriend is waiting for you!" Mom put her hand over her heart. "That's sooooo nice of her."

"Mom, not right now, please," I begged.

Mom rolled her eyes. "Well, okay. But I do want to have her over sometime!"

I took my time getting out of the car, and when I turned around, Grace was right next to me, holding her arms out for support. I glanced at Mom, who put her hand over her heart again and smiled at Grace. I shot Mom a look, and she took the hint. She gave me one last wave and drove off, probably thinking about how Grace and I would get married someday.

"I can carry those for you, Matt," Grace offered. She pushed her hair back and extended her arms like a walking zombie. She was being extremely nice, but I didn't want anyone from the soccer team to think I was terribly injured. If Coach Cup found out, then I wouldn't get to play in any games before the tournament. It was better that I acted tough or else my soccer season would be over.

"Thanks anyway, Grace. I think I can manage it," I said and patted her on the shoulder. I stood up straight and tried not to limp as I walked through the hallway with Grace to English class.

She was still ticked off at the lifeguard from the Montrose Pool who blamed me for the accident. "I'm telling you: those lifeguards have no idea what they're doing. They have no medical training, no common sense, and I bet they didn't even graduate high school!"

Listening to Grace complain was comforting. I laughed when she said that the lifeguard should quit his job and join the circus.

"I mean *seriously!* Who does that? Who puts the blame on the person who almost drowned?!" she continued.

We both exchanged a smile, and for the time being, Grace and I were getting along.

We got to English class and took our seats on opposite sides of the room while Mrs. Grubbles introduced our new book assignment for class. Mrs. Grubbles reminded me of the older ladies at my church, because she seemed to wear the same outfit all the time. She was short and round and each day wore sweaters with a giant animal stitched on them, like a giraffe or zebra. That day, her sweater had a picture of an enormous panda sitting next to a tree, and the class giggled each time she moved her arms, because it stretched the panda's face.

Something amazing happened as she started talking that day too. My body, which had spent all night trying to fall asleep, began to feel heavy. I sank further into my seat each passing minute that Mrs. Grubbles talked. I could feel myself relaxing. My hands folded underneath the desk. My head moved side to side. My eyes rolled in and out of my head. I was falling asleep.

My conscience sparked me, and I sat up quickly before I dozed off. I tried fighting off the sleepiness for most of the class, but as soon as Mrs. Grubbles started reading the beginning of our new book, my body zonked out and I fell asleep on my desk.

While Mrs. Grubbles read to the class, I had the most incredible and realistic dream! I dreamed I was walking on water but playing soccer at the same time. The crystal-clear water went as far as I could see, and I was the only one there. Each time I kicked the ball, water would splash, and I could even feel the drops of water hit my face. Even stranger, each time water hit me, I wouldn't get wet. I could plunge deep into the water with the ball and then rise to the top and run like it was hard ground. The entire dream, it was just me playing soccer on the ocean.

Everything seemed so clear and real that when Mrs. Grubbles woke me up, I thought the dream had actually happened.

"Matt? Matt Sprouts!" Mrs. Grubbles grunted.

My body lunged forward at the sudden sound of her

voice, and the class laughed while I massaged my eye sockets to keep them open.

"Oh, good. You're awake. Maybe you'd like to join us in our reading now, Mr. Sprouts?"

I shook my body to try to wake myself up even more and apologized to the teacher. "Yes, sorry, Mrs. Grubbles. I'm just really tired. I'll catch up in the reading."

"Yes, you will," she replied. "You'll be in lunch detention today to finish the reading you missed while napping. I hope it was worth it." She turned her back to me and started writing the assignment on the board for the rest of the class.

I'd never received detention before, and my tiredness quickly turned to anger at the thought of having to tell Mom and Dad what had happened. How come something bad *always* happened after I broke a toe? My anger boiled inside, and I couldn't control it. I let it loose on Mrs. Grubbles.

"Your panda sweater is the ugliest thing I've ever seen," I muttered—well, it actually wasn't a mutter. It was more like a shout.

Everyone in the class turned toward me and went, "Oooooooooh!" including Grace, who smiled a bit. Mrs. Grubbles didn't find it entertaining and slammed her marker down onto the whiteboard ledge. I was in serious trouble.

"Excuse me?" She took out another pink detention slip. "Well, I think you've earned yourself *another* detention today," Mrs. Grubbles said proudly.

Now, I'm not sure what caused the next event, but I do know it *wasn't* my fault.

As Mrs. Grubbles sat down to fill out my detention slip, her butt missed the chair, and she fell on her hip. The class immediately erupted in laughter, and some kids started acting out the fall on their own desk while Mrs. Grubbles lay on the floor. One kid stood on his desk and announced, "Look at me! I'm a panda, and I can't get up!" He jumped off the desk and rolled on the floor, and the class laughed even louder than the first time.

But everyone stopped in their tracks when Mrs. Grubbles started moaning for help. A girl ran to the office and brought back the school nurse, who then sat down next to Mrs. Grubbles on the floor.

"What happened to her?" the nurse asked our class. She scanned her head back and forth in search of an answer, but we stayed silent. "Really? No one has anything to say about this? Fine. Please grab your things and go to your next class."

Everyone walked past Mrs. Grubbles on their way out, but I made sure to stay toward the back of the line. When it was my turn to pass the door, I could see her eyes were closed and squinted, like she was in pain, and I think everyone felt a sense of guilt for making fun of her. I glanced at her desk and saw the pink detention slips, but they weren't filled out. Grace, who was right behind me, noticed too.

"If they aren't filled out, you don't have to go. That's what I say," she announced.

How could I argue with that? I took one last look at Mrs. Grubbles, who was sitting up and talking to the nurse now, and I walked out the door with Grace. Hopefully, Mrs. Grubbles would be okay.

The rest of the day was difficult for me. I practically had to pinch myself every time I wanted to fall asleep, and my toes were aching after walking in the boot. At the end of the day, I walked outside of the school into the pouring rain while Mom pulled up in the car. Deep puddles had already formed in the parking lot, and my boot got soaked while I tried to hop over them. I reached the car, but there was not one dry spot on me. I wished I was back in the dream I'd had earlier, where water didn't get me wet, not matter how much I played in it.

I got in the car next to Elliott, who must have avoided the rain, because he was perfectly dry. I shook my head like a dog and shot water droplets over him before he could protect himself.

"Hey!" Elliott pouted. "Knock it off! Mooommm!"

"Matt, stop it, okay?" Mom lectured. "I'm know you're still upset from yesterday, but don't take it out on your brother. You'll have plenty of time to rest tonight anyway—soccer practice was canceled."

"Sorry, Mom. Sorry, Elliott," I said under my breath.

Elliott turned and stuck his tongue out at me, then folded his arms together and looked out the window.

Mom started the car and began the drive home, but not

before handing me a card. "Here you go, Matt. This came in the mail for you today. Thought you might like it now instead of waiting to get it at home."

I figured it was a late birthday card from a relative or maybe something from Coach Cup, but it wasn't. The envelope was blank, except for my name on the front.

"How did this get to our mailbox? It doesn't even have an address on it," I asked.

"Just open it, Matt!" Elliott said from the side seat. His curiosity had gotten the best of him, and he didn't seem mad anymore. His head was practically in my lap.

I tore open the envelope and pulled out a green piece of folded construction paper. I flipped it open; loose pictures spilled out like confetti. Some were cut out of magazines and books, but two were hand drawn with black marker and pencil on the actual card, and they were really good!

Mom started to say, "Oh, that's thoughtful," but I didn't hear the rest. I couldn't stop looking at the words in the card, and Mom's voice just became white noise. I barely believed it. Jenna had actually made me a card, and it was the highlight of my day. The whole way home, while the thunder clapped and the car tires flipped water in the air, I could only stare at that card.

Suddenly, I didn't feel like a kid who had the Curse or a kid who'd almost gotten detention twice. Instead, I felt like I was ready to tackle the world, broken toes and all. I could do anything. Maybe Jenna's card would actually break the Curse. I mean, she'd forgiven me, right? I thought of soccer and knew I could play, even if it meant lying to Coach Cup and playing with two broken toes. I could do it. I could beat the Curse.

I went to bed early that night. I placed Jenna's card on my dartboard in front of my bed so I could see it. Jenna must have known cards had the power to heal, because my mind was at rest and my body felt ready for the next week. I dozed off to sleep while looking at the card from my bed and had one of the best nights of sleep ever.

I'd have to tell Jenna the next time we talked.

CHAPTER 16
THE GOLDEN DRESS

I woke up Saturday with a sense of determination. It was the middle of September, which meant I had about one month left of soccer practice before the Turkey Shoot-Out Soccer Tournament at the end of October. I knew Coach Cup wouldn't play me in the tournament if I missed a month of practice, so I needed a way to bandage up the toes so I could play. Saturday's mission, then, was to find a solution to the Curse.

I went straight to Mom's room to root through all of her arts-and-crafts materials. I hoped to find something to cushion my toes in my cleat, but before I got to the room, Mom stopped me in the hallway.

"Here, hold these and follow me. I need help with costume design," she said and handed me a large cardboard box. Costume design. I knew right away what that meant.

So . . . I've been hiding something that I don't like to talk about much. Mom owns a dance studio where she teaches tap, jazz, and ballet classes to hundreds of squirrely little kids. This wouldn't be an issue if she didn't constantly keep asking Elliott and me to take a ballet class. I mean, I tried ballet class once, and it wasn't horrible. I guess soccer is just my thing and dance, well, isn't. Plus, I don't want to dance with Elliott. I'd rather fight a gorilla.

Costume design, though, is something I couldn't get out of.

Mom always made the costumes (fluffy blue tutus, pink-striped skirts, green velvet dresses) for her dance recitals each year. Making one dress to hold up and look at isn't enough for her, though. Nope, Mom needs a real model—someone to try it on and do a few spins to see how it looks. That "someone" who has to try them on each year is me. Mom calls it "costume design." I call it "torture."

She led me to the kitchen where more boxes of sparkly gold dresses sat. Just seeing them put me in a bad mood.

"Mom, this is silly. Can't you just have one of your students try them on?" I begged.

"If I did that, I would have to wait till Monday, Matt. I want to see how they look now. Here, take this. I think it will fit." She handed me what she called "a size six" and told me to put it on.

"How many times do I have to do this?" I asked. "Shouldn't Dad take a turn?"

"Haha," Mom mocked sarcastically. "Make sure you don't rip the leggings when you pull them up."

I stripped down to my shorts and pulled the flowing gold dress on. It was itchy, uncomfortable, and awkward. I stood there with my arms at my hips, frowning so hard my face hurt. It wasn't the dress itself. It was Mom making me wear something I didn't want to wear.

"Do a spin," Mom said with her hand on her chin, as if she were studying a masterpiece. "I want to see how it looks when it moves."

"Oooooh! You look very spinny!" Elliott was hiding on the sofa in the living room and picked his head up, which was resting in a half-empty bowl of cereal.

"Knock it off, Elliott! Or I'll punch you!" I yelled.

"Boys! Stop it," Mom intervened. "Okay, Matt, you can take it off. Thanks for your help."

I yanked the dress off and put my shirt back on as I walked back to Mom's room. I got down on my stomach and pulled myself under Mom and Dad's bed, where Mom kept all her arts-and-crafts materials. I pushed aside some dusty cardboard boxes until I found the woven basket. I scooted backward and pulled the basket out with me, then began rooting through the materials to find something that could help protect my toes.

Most of what Mom had were sewing needles and bits of string, but I did find some things that looked helpful. There were some large white cotton balls, thick multicolored yarn, and clear duct tape. I didn't exactly know what I was going to do with it yet, but I shoved it all in the pockets of my shorts and ran to my room to get my soccer cleats. It was time to experiment.

For the next hour, I tried to find ways to make my soccer cleat more comfortable. First, I tried wrapping the yarn around my toes to see whether that helped the pain. Nope, no luck. I tried taping the toes tighter together. Nope, no luck there either. In a last-ditch effort, I threw all the cotton balls inside the cleat, wrapped the yarn around my toes, and stuck it together with the clear tape. It took me a minute to wiggle and weave my foot into the shoe, but it finally slid in.

I stood up and took a few steps. No pain. I jogged around my room a few times. No pain!

For the final test, I took a soccer ball out of my closet and started kicking it off the wall with my large cottoned left foot.

"Matt, what's all that noise?!" Dad yelled from the other side of the house.

"Sorry, Dad! I'm done now!" I hollered back.

There was virtually no pain. A few cotton balls, some bits of yarn, and some tape completed Saturday's mission.

By Monday, my broken toes would be ready for soccer practice. I quickly took my other cleat and shoveled in more string and tape. All that cushion would hopefully protect me from another attack of the Curse.

I was so excited I *had* to share the news with someone, so I called Eric. He answered right away.

"Hey, Matt," Eric said, almost annoyed.

"Hey, Eric! Did Jenna give you my message earlier? Doesn't matter, though. I fixed my toes, and I'll be able to play next week!" I was proud of my fix-it job, and the joy was practically pouring out of me.

Eric's response was less than enthusiastic. "Uh-huh. I've got some friends over. Is there something else you want?"

I was a little shocked. "Um, I guess not. Want to hang out later today?" I could hear laughter in the background.

"Nah. See ya," Eric said and hung up the phone.

I stood there with the phone at my side. I didn't understand. Ever since school had started, it seemed like Eric was doing his best to avoid me. Even in the one class we had together, woodshop, it was like I wasn't there. He always partnered with someone else and never even said hi to me at the beginning of class. If it weren't for soccer practice forcing Eric to play with me, I probably wouldn't see him at all during the week.

Still, I had to share my accomplishment with somebody—anybody. So I went to Elliott's room. He was sitting on the floor playing with some action figures, but he was also wearing my favorite hockey shirt. Not cool.

"Hey, why are you wearing my shirt?" I was mad already, but I tried my best to be polite.

"It's not your shirt. It's mine. Aunt Ann gave it to me last year," Elliott stated while keeping his eyes on his wrestling action figures.

But we both knew it wasn't his. Last year before my birthday, Mom secretly told her sister, Aunt Ann, that I really liked hockey. And since Aunt Ann is the coolest person you will ever meet, she bought me a limited-edition hockey shirt of the Colorado Blizzards, my favorite hockey team! Everyone knew it was my favorite shirt. I mean, everyone. And that included Elliott.

"Um . . . are you serious? I wear that shirt almost every day!" I barked. It was true too. The hockey shirt and my gray sweatpants were my favorite outfit to wear. I wasn't the trendiest kid in school, but maybe Elliott was starting to like my style.

"It's mine," Elliott said. "Get out of my room with your soccer cleats!"

With my cleats still on, I ran up to Elliott and started pulling the shirt off. Elliott fought back with more force than I expected, and I tumbled to the ground next to him. I kept my grip on the shirt and pinned Elliott to the ground with my other hand. I took a few swings at his head but missed, so I dug my elbow into the side of his face and squished it into the carpet.

At this point, Elliott did what he did best: cried. It was his last line of defense, but it always worked to get Mom's or Dad's attention. I jumped to my feet, and he pulled off *my* shirt and threw it.

"Just take the shirt! I don't want it anyway!" he cried and ran off toward the living room.

I grabbed the shirt and stuffed it in my dresser, where hopefully he wouldn't find it again. Elliott was crying, but I was a little shaken up too. We'd never actually gotten in a physical fight like that before. Most of our fights followed the same pattern: I'd push Elliott, he'd cry, and then our parents would show up. But this time was much different. We never wrestled like that, and Elliott was really upset.

I took my cleats off and sat them at the edge of my bed. Mom entered the room with the box of golden dresses.

"What happened with you and Elliott?" she asked.

I could tell she already blamed me for it, but I wasn't going to let Elliott get away scot-free.

"Elliott was wearing one of my shirts and wouldn't take it off, and he started fighting me," I said. The sentence was simple enough to put the blame on Elliott—and off of me. I hoped.

"Well, I got a much different story from Elliott, which means you're both to blame."

I kept my head down so I wouldn't have to look Mom in the eyes while she talked.

"You know, Matt, your brother really looks up to you, a lot more than you think he does. Sometimes, little brothers just want to be like the people they admire, even if that means dressing like them."

"But he *always* takes my stuff!" I said in defense.

"Even so, did you ever think that Elliott is lonely after the summer? You two see each other most of the summer, and then you're off doing soccer and other things. You barely see him during the school year."

I stayed silent.

"You're not in trouble, Matt; just know that Elliott enjoys you as a brother. Now, I need you to try on another dress. This time, a size seven. I'll meet you in the kitchen in a few minutes." She tossed the dress to me, and it fluttered down onto the edge of my bed.

As I squeezed into the sparkly dress, I thought about what she had said. It was true—Elliott and I had spent almost the entire summer together at the Klinkles' house, and now I saw him only in the car and at dinner. We didn't have time to play together at all, and as much as I hated to admit it, I missed his dorky face.

It made me think about Eric too. Since the summer, he'd basically disappeared from my life, and I didn't like losing my best friend. If Elliott felt at all about me the way I did about Eric, then I needed to apologize to him.

I shuffled in the dress across the carpeted hallway and into the kitchen. Some shimmering light passed through the sliding glass door from the living room, and I moved the curtains to get a better look. Elliott was sitting on the patio in a golden dress with his baggy black shorts hanging out the bottom. His arms were folded over his knees, his face looking toward the mountains. I guess he was finally old enough to suffer through helping Mom with costume design. I was no longer alone.

I snagged two ice pops from the fridge and sat down next to Elliott on the patio. He didn't move or look at me.

"Hey," I muttered. I searched deep inside myself for something meaningful to say, but nothing came to mind, so I just let my lips run without planning anything first. "I'm really sorry, Elliott. I'm just upset about my toes and all."

He huffed but didn't say anything else, so I kept going.

"I guess I'm also mad that we don't get to hang out as much as we did during the summer. We're both so busy. Stinks, doesn't it?"

Elliott finally spoke. "Yeah, it stinks," he grumbled.

"Well, maybe you and I can hang out during the weekend, when I don't have soccer practice and stuff? What do you think?" I offered.

Elliott turned his head and searched my eyes with his. I think he was trying to figure out whether I was serious. I was serious, and Elliott would have known if I was lying.

"Yeah, that'd be good," he sniffled.

I handed him an ice pop, and we ate them together, watching the llamas eat hay in the pasture against the backdrop of the beautiful mountain sky.

"How's the dress feel?" I asked.

"Horrible. I hate it. How many times do we have to do this?" he asked.

"Probably until the day we die. Or until we get so big we can't fit anything else on."

We both laughed and started doing impressions of dancers on the porch. Elliott did a waltz, and I acted like I was tapping with my good foot, letting the broken toes take a rest. When Mom came out, we were laughing so loud she had to yell to get our attention.

"You both get back inside before you ruin those! I can't afford for you two to be getting those dresses all dirty!"

We stood up, and on the way inside, Elliott brought up the Curse.

"So do you think it's real now, Matt?"

Despite him being a blabbermouth, I gave him a truthful answer. "Yeah, I do."

He nodded, and we walked inside to see Dad sitting on the couch with a tray full of nachos. He smirked and asked, "Those look a little big. I think you should try on all the other sizes, just to make sure you find one that fits just right. Don't you?"

Elliott and I looked at each other, smiled, then charged at Dad. He had just enough time to put the tray down before we tackled him and tried to give him wet willies in his ear. He threw us both up on the couch, and we laughed and tried again. Mom raised her voice again and said we were going to rip her costumes, but we kept going anyway.

It was the last time I'd have to try on a dress for Mom— or anyone, for that matter. I think she realized I was too much of a hassle and that Elliott could do it from now on. Elliott and I spent the rest of the weekend together, playing in the backyard with Nala, swimming in the creek, and watching ninja movies at night in my room.

It was the best weekend I'd had in a while.

CHAPTER 17
RETURN OF THE PURPLE GRAPE

I didn't wear the boot to school on Monday. Of course, Mom and Dad didn't know that. As soon as Mom dropped me off at school, I switched to my soccer cleats in my gym bag. I couldn't risk anyone on the soccer team thinking I was injured, and if Coach Cup heard from another player that I was hurt, then soccer would be over. So I did the only thing I could think of: I wore my soccer cleats to school. But this ended up drawing more attention than wearing a boot. Grace was the first to notice.

"What are you doing?" Grace looked around and pulled me close to her locker. "You are going to embarrass us! My boyfriend can't be seen with cleats on in school. It'll make us look bad!"

"Grace, you're not my girl—" I decided not to fight about the fake girlfriend/boyfriend thing. It just didn't seem worth it at the moment. Grace was so stubborn anyway that if I did argue with her, it would cost me a load of trouble. I tried to change the subject. "I've been meaning to ask you: Why are you sticking with me? Haven't you heard? I'm the boy with the Curse! Shouldn't you be, like, running to find another fake boyfriend?"

Grace just smiled. "I know. I'm not worried. Plus, maybe I don't want a different fake boyfriend."

Um, what? Was Grace trying to tell me something? I decided not to read too much into it.

"Look, it doesn't really matter," I said. "And no one will notice my cleats. Anyway, do you think Mrs. Grubbles will be teaching today?"

My question easily distracted Grace from my stuffed cleats. "Oh! I heard she is on medical leave and she won't be back for a month. I bet we have a substitute today," she guessed, and we started our walk toward English class.

For a substitute, trying to take control of a sixth-grade class for a month would be like trying to teach an entire country a different language. The sub would have no idea what was going on, and since Mrs. Grubbles probably hadn't had time to write lessons while she'd been lying on the floor of the classroom with a bruised hip, the sub would have nothing to hold over our heads. No homework, no projects, nothing. English class was going to be a cinch.

Grace and I entered the class and took our seats, but there was no teacher in sight. Kids were scattered around the room, some sitting on Mrs. Grubbles's desk, others playing cards on the floor. Henry and John spotted us from the front and came over to chat.

"This is so cool!" John exclaimed. "It's been five minutes, and we still don't have a teacher!"

"Yeah!" Henry added. "And so far, no homework for us!"

I extended his hand for a high five, but Grace beat me to it and smacked Henry's hand so hard he had to shake it to cool it off.

While Henry rubbed his hand from Grace's painful high five, Principal Oriano walked through the doorway and whistled. Everyone at school knew not to mess with Principal O. He was over six and a half feet tall and built out of pure muscle. If he wanted to, he could challenge the entire class to tug-of-war and still easily win. After Principal O.'s whistle, everyone took their seats immediately without a snicker of laughter.

"Thank you," Principal O. announced. "Now, I know you've been wondering about Mrs. Grubbles, and I'm sure you've all heard different rumors. Well, you can squash all those rumors now, because Mrs. Grubbles will be just fine. She is going to take some time off to rest, but she said she'll miss you all and see you after she heals up."

Grace raised her hand and, in her usual suck-up voice, asked the obvious question on everyone's mind: "So, Principal O., who will be taking her spot?"

"Good question, Grace," Principal O. said. "Your substitute actually used to teach in this very building and was around when this school was first built. Can you believe that, kids?"

"I'm not *that* old!" screeched a voice from the hallway. The sound of high heels clicking on tile filled the room, and a purple cane emerged from the hallway. It was followed by a pair of purple shoes, and attached to the purple shoes were purple pants connected to a sparkly purple jacket. I recognized the faded purple design right away. I didn't even need to see her face to know whom I would be spending the next month with. I slid low in my seat and propped an open book on my desk so I couldn't be seen. The sub was the old grape lady.

"Ah! There you are. So glad you could make it on such short notice today," Principal O. said as he helped her to Mrs. Grubbles's desk.

The old grape lady smiled through her crooked glasses. I stayed low and kept my face behind the book. If she recognized me from the summer, my life would be over.

"Class, I would like to introduce your substitute teacher for the next couple months," Principal O. announced. "This is Mrs. Klinkle."

My ears wiggled. Mrs. Klinkle? As in Mr. Klinkle's wife? The lady Elliott and I never saw? No. Couldn't be. What were the chances of that?! I peered around the pages of my book to get a better glimpse. Mrs. Klinkle was unpacking her purple bag, spilling pages and binders all over Mrs. Grubbles's desk.

Principal O. seemed satisfied and started walking out the door. "Well, I guess I'll let you do your teaching, Mrs. Klinkle. Let me know if you need anything."

Mrs. Klinkle ignored him and continued dumping her belongings onto the desk. With her back turned to us as she rooted through the papers, she started talking.

"Now, I don't want any funny business this month. Understand? I know you think I'm a tiny old lady who doesn't know squat, but you *will* pay attention during class, and you *will* learn what I teach. When you walk out of this room, you'll thank me for what you've learned. Is that clear?"

The class was shocked by her sudden demands and didn't say a thing.

"Is. That. Clear?" Mrs. Klinkle said, raising her voice and taking her first, hard look at the class.

Yeses slowly and quietly emerged from the kids around the room, but I kept my mouth shut behind my book.

"All right, then." Mrs. Klinkle cleared her throat and slammed a large dusty binder onto the desk. "Today, we will be reading about the great pyramids of Egypt. There will be a short quiz tomorrow and a test on Friday, so I suggest you all pay attention." There was a short pause in her voice. "And that includes you too, Matt Sprouts. Put that book down."

I could feel the blood drain from my face as I lowered the book. How did she know my name?

"Ah, thank you, Matt. You look much different in a desk than with piles of rocks around you." Mrs. Klinkle adjusted her glasses. "Now, sit up and pay attention."

It was official. Mrs. Klinkle was the old grape lady. If the class knew what I knew about her, they would have a reason to be as nervous as I was. I had to tell Eric about this, even if he brushed me off afterward.

The bell rang shortly after Mrs. Klinkle introduced Greek and Latin roots, which took almost thirty minutes. When I got up to leave, Mrs. Klinkle made an announcement to the class, but it was directed at me. I could tell.

"Study tonight, students. Oh, and, class, please don't wear soccer cleats to school. It looks foolish, and it's against the student code of conduct," Mrs. Klinkle said while looking directly at me.

I felt the blood return to my face, and I blushed as the entire class stared at my puffy left cleat. At this rate, English class was going to be horrible for the next month.

🔆

I arrived at soccer practice with every intent of telling Eric how Mrs. Klinkle was actually the old grape lady, but when I saw him surrounded by his seventh-grade buddies, I got nervous and decided to save it for another time when Eric was alone. I sat on the bench and took out some more cotton balls from my backpack and shoved them in my cleat. The cotton balls and yarn helped, but I could still feel the pinching nerves throughout my toes. It was going to be a hard practice, but if I could get through it, I could get through the rest of the month. I had to. The Curse could not win.

Coach Cup started us off with field sprints. He blew his whistle, and we all sprinted toward the other goal. Even though the team was a mix of sixth and seventh graders, I was still one of the fastest kids on the field. I made it to the goal line first and bent down to catch my breath. Running seemed relatively pain free, but kicking the ball would be the real test of my strength.

We ran for the next ten minutes before Coach Reese called us over for some passing work. I grabbed a ball with my hands and carried it over toward the center of the field. Everyone seemed to have a partner already, except for Eric, who was trying to join another group of two.

"Eric! Have you lost your brain?!" Coach Cup yelled from the sideline. "Matt's been standing right behind you with no partner! Do I have to draw you a map, or can you get there by yourself?!"

Eric rolled his eyes. "Let's get this over with," he said and faced me with a disgusted look.

I dropped the ball to the ground and took a swing with my left foot. I wanted to throw my cleat off and dunk my foot in a bucket of ice right away, but Dad's words played like music and scrolling news in my head: "You can't let those curveballs bother you either. You have to tackle those problems, confront them head-on."

Those words were enough to keep me from collapsing. Eric skipped the ball back to me, so I gritted my teeth together and gave the ball another kick. It was painful but

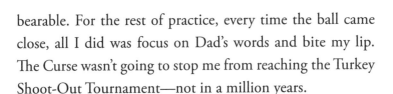

bearable. For the rest of practice, every time the ball came close, all I did was focus on Dad's words and bite my lip. The Curse wasn't going to stop me from reaching the Turkey Shoot-Out Tournament—not in a million years.

At the end of practice Coach Cup gathered the team and announced that we had only one game left before the tournament and that our next game would determine how we fit in the bracket. If we won, we would play an easier team in the first round. If we lost, we would play the number one team in the bracket, Eagle Crest, who had beaten us earlier in the year.

Coach Reese made the final point before practice ended: "The game is going to be against Mountain View Academy this Saturday. Get some rest for practice this week, boys, because we are going to hit it hard! See you all tomorrow."

When I got home that night, I went straight to the closet and got the cleaning bucket to fill it with cold water. We didn't have any ice in the freezer, so I grabbed a package of frozen peas and carrots and tossed it in the water to cool it off. I sat in my room with my toes in the bucket and waited to tell Elliott about my day. As soon as he got home from piano lessons, I called him to my room. He entered holding his dinner plate filled with leftover mashed potatoes and chicken, and it made me realize how hungry I was. It was Dad's night to cook, which usually ends with us all choosing leftovers instead of whatever disaster he made. I had totally forgotten, and Elliott had already grabbed the best leftover meal in the house. A peanut-butter-and-jelly sandwich would have to do for me, because I was not gonna eat whatever Dad slopped together.

Elliott sat on the edge of my bed and laughed while I told him all about the old grape lady being Mrs. Klinkle. As usual, he asked a bunch of questions I didn't have the answers to, but it was nice spending time with Elliott.

"So do you think she'll know it was you who honked the horn during the summer?" Elliott asked.

I adjusted my foot in the bucket. "I hope not. She didn't say anything about it when I saw her. Maybe she forgot."

"Yeah, right!" Elliott chuckled. "She's probably waiting for the right second to spit at you again!"

The image of that suggestion grossed me out, so I changed the subject. "Are there any more mashed potatoes left in the fridge? I'm starving."

"No, but you can have some of mine," Elliott offered.

"Really? Can I?"

"Sure," he said and scraped the rest of his mashed potatoes into the ice bucket and ran out of the room laughing.

We might have bonded over the golden dresses, but we were still brothers. I'd have to get him back another day, when my toes were fully healed. I pulled my foot out of the mushy mashed potato ice water and stared at my swollen toes. Until they healed, I'd just have to focus on the soccer game and try to get through English class without Mrs. Klinkle spitting on me.

CHAPTER 18
THE READING

The rest of the week was pretty tough leading up to the soccer game. My toes were still swollen, and the cushions in my soccer cleats helped take the pain down only a tiny bit. Mrs. Klinkle wasn't making life easier either. She must have been trained at a military academy, because she caught every little thing that happened in the classroom, even when she wasn't there. For example, on Tuesday we had a quiz about Latin roots (which I managed to squeeze a C+ out of), but in the middle of the quiz, Mrs. Klinkle stepped into the hallway to talk to Principal O. Meanwhile, Janet, one of Grace's friends, raced to the front of the room to steal the answers on the desk, then ran back and sat down before Mrs. Klinkle came back in.

"Who was at my desk?" Mrs. Klinkle yelled. "Who was it?!" She scanned the room, pointing at every kid. Her finger stopped on Janet, who immediately turned red.

"It was *you*," Mrs. Klinkle chuckled with a sinister grin. She walked up to Janet's desk, picked up her test, and tore it in half from top to bottom. "Let this be a lesson to all of you: don't you *ever* cheat in this room."

Janet broke down into tears immediately, and I blame her for my C+, because she cried the rest of the period and I couldn't focus.

Mrs. Klinkle also had lockable eyes. I don't know how she did it, but any time she lectured on proper sentences or punctuation format, her eyes focused on me. Even when she handed out papers or wrote on the board, her head would swivel and her eyes would find me.

Turns out I wasn't the only one feeling this way. I told Grace about the teacher's creepy stares, but she disagreed and said, "No way! She stares at *me* the whole time! How could she stare at *you*?"

I polled the rest of the class later that day, and although it doesn't make any sense, every kid thought Mrs. Klinkle was looking at them. What kind of teacher is able to strike fear into everyone she looks at? Mrs. Klinkle sure knew how to keep a class of kids on the edge of their seats, and she really had my attention on Tuesday.

"Mr. Sprouts, will you read section 1.5 on the pyramids aloud for the class?"

"Yes," I grumbled and began, "'The great pyramids of Egypt are known mostly for their architecture, but little do people understand about the history of curses said to roam the tombs of the pharaohs.'" I stopped reading and stared at the word *curses*.

"Please continue, Mr. Sprouts. You might learn a thing or two," Mrs. Klinkle scowled.

I gulped and went on, "'The curses are said to fall upon anyone who enters the pyramids uninvited or who breaks something of importance. Since they did something bad, they've been cursed. Some who claim they are cursed become fixated on it and drive themselves mad. Others say they have beaten the curse by conquering quests, defeating foes, or winning something important . . .'"

A kid spoke up from the back of the room. "Hey, Sprouts! Is this written about you?!" The rest of the class burst into laughter, and even Mrs. Klinkle snorted a chuckle.

I stopped reading. Was this some sort of sign? Was the Curse taunting me, or was this a hint that I could actually break the Curse? I could feel my heart skip a beat as I thought of the possibility of being free from my torment.

"Fine! I'll continue reading, since Mr. Sprouts obviously can't," Mrs. Klinkle announced, but I was in a trance.

While her squawky voice filled the classroom, I made a decision: if people in Egypt had beaten curses, so could I. The school textbook said that Egyptians had to complete something like a quest or mission, but I couldn't think of anything in my life even close to a mission. Maybe I had to beat someone up or win something big . . .

And that's when it hit me: I didn't have any enemies,

quests, or missions, but I did have one thing I could win that seemed impossible, and it was big—so big that the Curse would definitely leave if I won: the Turkey Shoot-Out Tournament. It was my only way to break the Curse.

The next day I decided the best thing for me to do was keep my mouth shut unless Mrs. Klinkle called on me again. As long as she didn't recognize me from the summer drive, I could get through the class without any more problems. All I had to do was complete the work she asked and concentrate on my new goal of beating the Curse. I needed to win the upcoming Turkey Shoot-Out Tournament.

Grace wasn't causing many problems, either, and we were getting along pretty well after Mrs. Klinkle took over. Occasionally, Grace would hug me in the hall (it always felt warm and cozy, like a soft, heavy blanket) or announce to Henry and John that we would "get married someday," but all in all, she wasn't as scary as she used to be. I even decided to invite her bee catching with Henry, John, and me at recess on Wednesday, but that didn't go over so well.

"You're going to kill all of them! Stop it! You're so mean!" Grace yelled as she tried to shepherd the bees away from us.

John tried to talk her out of it, but Grace's bossy voice was too much for him to handle. "My boyfriend is not going to be some bee killer. Got it, John?"

John was learning quickly that when Grace was mad, it was best not to say anything, but for some reason, he must have felt brave that day. So he talked back to her. "Matt isn't even your boyfriend, Grace. Snap out of it, why don't you—"

Grace walked up to John and poked him hard in the stomach. "Stay out of it, John. Got it?!"

Grace was kinda like my bodyguard: she had to know I was safe or else she would terrorize every person who came my way. But, I liked that about her. I liked a lot of things about her, actually. It was comforting knowing she had my back whenever I needed it, even if she did get a little unruly.

As I watched Grace threaten John, I suddenly realized . . . I actually liked Grace. And I wasn't faking it either.

"Grace! Hold on a second!" I was nervous. What was I going to say? I hadn't even planned anything!

She stepped away from John and looked at me. "What? Why are you staring at me like that?" One of her eyebrows raised like she was searching for a clue.

I gathered all the courage inside of me and just said it. "I like you. Will you be my girlfriend?"

There was a long pause. Or maybe it was short? I don't know, but it felt like forever.

Grace smiled, and her eyes beamed. "You aren't faking it, are you?"

"No way," I smiled back. "Are *you* faking it?"

"No, I haven't been faking it for a while!" She ran over, gave me a hug, and started screaming.

"Oh, I can't wait to tell everyone!" Grace clapped her hands together. "We are actually dating!"

Henry laughed. "Everyone already knows you're dating, Grace. You've been telling the whole school since day one!"

John and I laughed too, because it was true. Me asking Grace to be my girlfriend wouldn't really change anything, except maybe holding her hand more often. And I was looking forward to that.

Finally agreeing to be Grace's boyfriend actually created some problems, though. She was even clingier than before, and kids at school noticed. She called me each night to talk on the phone, and she showed up to all my soccer practices the rest of the week, which made me an easy target for Coach Cup.

"Who's that little girl sitting in the bleachers waving at you, Sprouts? That your sister?" Coach Cup cackled while we were stretching.

"No, just a girl from school," I said. I didn't want to deny it, but I didn't know how Coach would react if he knew.

"That's his girlfriend, Coach!" someone blurted out from across the circle. It was Eric, and he was grinning quite mischievously.

"Ohhhh, I see." Coach Cup walked up behind me and slapped my back with his clipboard. "I didn't know you were dating an elf." Coach Reese stepped in to break it up before I said anything stupid.

"Knock it off, Coach Cup, and let's get these kids focused on the game, all right?"

While Coach Cup talked about the strategy to beat

Mountain View Academy, I glared at Eric, who didn't seem to care that he humiliated me in front of the whole team. Did he do that on purpose? Why was he being such a scumbag? What had I done to him anyway? I decided that sooner rather than later, I'd have to talk to him, whether he wanted to or not. Somehow, I'd get him to spill it.

And he did—just not at the time or in the place I thought he would.

CHAPTER 19
BREAKING THE CURSE

It was Saturday and time for our last soccer game against Mountain View before the Turkey Shoot-Out Tournament. I had enough cotton balls and yarn to get me through the game. This was my first chance to break the Curse. If we could beat Mountain View, it would set us up for a better chance at winning the tournament—and a better chance to break the Curse.

Mom and Dad were excited for the game too, and cooked a large French toast breakfast for Elliott and me before we got in the car to leave for Summit Hill.

Summit Hill is the best place for soccer games. It's on top of a ridge that overlooks the town, and it seems like someone carved the soccer field into the mountain just for us. It is surrounded by pine and aspen trees and has a few small ponds just beyond the concession stands. With the ponds, the ducks and geese get a free front-row seat to watch us play, which makes Summit Hill kind of a paradise for any soccer fan.

When I got to the field, Coach Cup handed the team our new white-and-red jerseys, and we started our normal warm-up routine. We jogged around the field and passed the Mountain View team, who didn't seem threatened by our new jerseys. They were a larger team but nothing we couldn't handle on the soccer field.

We ran by the stands too, where I saw the Monkling family sitting next to mine. Jenna was the first to spot me, and she waved. It was good to see Jenna there, so before I forgot, I yelled out, "Thanks for the card! It really helped!" Jenna gave me a thumbs-up, then turned toward Eric to cheer him on.

John, Henry, and Grace were sitting at the very top behind my parents and Elliott. I could hear Grace's deafening voice explaining the rules of the game to Henry, who wasn't really a sports guy.

"And that's the goalkeeper. His job is to keep the ball from getting in the net," Grace lectured. "It is one of the hardest positions to play and—Matt! Over here!"

I waved as we jogged past, and Grace stopped her lecture and stood up to blow me a kiss. I could feel my face blush, and John and Henry both cracked up while Grace called out "Good luck!" from the stands.

As the team stretched, Coach Cup reminded us how important the game was. If we won, we played an easier team first in the tournament. If we lost, we would play Eagle Crest first.

"I want you all to lock down on defense. Anytime they get the ball, I expect you all to sprint like your pants are on fire. Got it?"

We all nodded and joined hands, and Coach Reese got us started: "Montrose Mountaineers on three! One, two, three!"

We erupted in cheers and took our spots on the field. Coach Cup started me at midfield, while Eric sat the bench for the first part of the game. The ref blew the whistle, and Mountain View began their attack. For the first fifteen minutes of the game, Mountain View controlled the ball and took multiple shots on our goal. Thankfully, none of them went in, but they were getting closer with each shot, so we had to change the momentum of the game—fast.

Our goalie threw the ball out to me, and I bolted as fast as I could down the sideline. My toes were broken, but they held up strong enough to propel me down the field. I could hear Dad chanting as I passed the ball between two Mountain View defenders to one of my teammates, who took our first shot on goal. The ball clanged off the upper post and knocked out of bounds. So close!

The rest of the first half was back and forth between both teams, but neither of us could get a goal. We battled until the whistle blew for the end of the first half, then gathered around Coach Cup for any words of encouragement he might have—but he had none.

"Do you *want* to lose today?! Are you *trying* to embarrass yourselves?!" Coach Cup yelled as he flipped his clipboard over his back in the air. "Unbelievable!"

Coach Reese put his arm across Coach Cup's chest to calm him down.

"I think what Coach Cup is trying to say is that we need some more offensive attacks. We need to push the ball forward to get some more shots on goal. That's our mission for the next half, agreed? Mountaineers on three!"

We cheered and ran back on the field, but Coach Reese grabbed my shoulder before I left.

"Matt, I want you to play forward. We need some more speed up there, okay? See whether you can make something happen. Please."

I jumped at the opportunity and shook Coach Reese's hand with a firm grip of determination. "You got it, Coach," I said and ran back to the field.

The start of the second half began just like the first. Mountain View controlled the game and trampled through our defense like it didn't exist. After only five minutes, a Mountain View forward weaved through our last defender and shot the ball in the bottom of the goal. Mountain View: 1, Montrose Mountaineers: 0.

I tried not to let it bother me. We still had plenty of time to even out the score, and we'd come from behind before. The ref brought the ball to the center of the field for a kickoff, and we began our attack on Mountain View. I used my speed to tire out their defenders, and after multiple runs down the sidelines with the ball, it was starting to work. I kept feeding the ball to the center of the field to our forwards, who had a couple good shots, but nothing went in the net. I glanced at the clock, and with only five minutes remaining, I was starting to feel the pressure. If we lost this game, breaking the Curse was going to be even harder.

After another missed shot on goal, Coach Cup yelled for a sub and sent Eric in for the final five minutes. Eric would have fresh legs, which meant we might be able to outhustle the defenders if we got the chance.

Mountain View put the ball back in play and raced down the field with it. They passed the ball back and forth between players, playing keep-away and letting the clock wind down. No one on our defense could get ahold of the ball, and I ran around, frantically trying to help in any way I could.

Finally, a Mountain View player passed the ball too softly, and our team intercepted it. The defender kicked the ball toward me, and I took off down the field. I easily outran the first defender and punted the ball to Eric, who was open in the middle of the field. He dodged another defender and sprinted toward the goal, with only one more defender separating him and the goalie.

I charged as fast as I could and followed Eric through the middle of the field. The Mountain View guard closed in on Eric, leaving me all alone in front of the net.

I yelled and clapped my hands for the ball. "Eric! Pass it now! I'm open! I'm open!"

Eric's eyes scanned me, but he kept going straight toward the defender.

"Eric! Quick!" I screamed, but it was too late.

The defender dropped to the ground and swiped the ball out from Eric's feet, stealing our last chance at a goal. The ref blew his whistle, and the game was suddenly over. Mountain View won, and my chances of breaking the broken-toe curse suddenly got much more complicated.

My emotions got the best of me, and I ran over to Eric, who was still on the ground by the goal.

"What is wrong with you? I was wide open! We could have scored!"

Eric fixed his crooked shin guard and tried to stand up. "Be quiet, Matt. Just shut it."

I wasn't going to put up with Eric's attitude this time, and I shoved him back to the grass. "No! Seriously, what's wrong with you? Ever since school started, you've been a jerk. You won't even talk to me! I haven't done anything to make you upset!"

He jumped to his feet and pushed me back. "Back off, Matt! You don't even know what you did!"

"How am I supposed to know if you won't tell me?" I yelled back. I could see Coach Reese running toward us to stop the fight.

"Fine! You really want to know? You stole Grace!" Eric shouted at me.

I was stumped. "What? Stole who?"

"I liked Grace, and you stole her from me!"

What?! Another curveball! How was I supposed to know Eric liked Grace? He never told me, and as far as I knew, he didn't even know Grace existed. It didn't make any sense.

Before I could finish processing what was going on, or tell him that Grace couldn't possibly be stolen because she did things on her own free will, Eric put his shoulder into my stomach and tackled me to the ground. Coach Reese yanked him off me and told him to sit on the bench. I rolled around on the ground for a minute to catch my breath. Coach helped me to my feet and brought me to the sideline next to Eric and the rest of the team.

Coach Cup was over in the parking lot, kicking the water cooler and swearing up a storm, so Coach Reese took control of the team.

"Look—I don't know what that fight was all about, but I do know we are all a little upset about the game. Here's what I want you all to do today: go home and get some rest, and next week we will prepare for our first tournament game against Eagle Crest. Just because we lost today doesn't mean we will lose again. Shake this one off, fellas, okay?"

We nodded and started taking off our shin guards and cleats, but Eric grabbed his bag and went toward his family in the bleachers without saying another word. Grace ran right past him on her way across the field and patted me on the back. "What was that about?"

"I'm not sure," I lied. "I think he's just mad about the game . . ."

My friendship with Eric had just gotten more complex, and it was going to take some work to repair the damage. Worse, my shot at breaking the Curse by winning the Turkey Shoot-Out was going to be ten times harder now that Eagle Crest was standing in our way.

CHAPTER 20
A WINDY
CONVERSATION

The wind whipped leaves against my bedroom window and beat the trees together, waking me up Sunday morning, the day after the game. It was October, and my life was more complicated than ever. I couldn't quite shake the broken-toe curse, Eric hated me, and I had an English teacher who despised me on every level imaginable. It was the absolute worst.

I snuggled into my warm sheets and smooshed my face in my pillow. I could feel my bloated toes underneath the cover of my bed, and I knew getting up meant facing the pain of walking. If it weren't for the smell of bacon in the kitchen, I would have stayed in bed all day.

I moseyed out of my room and let the smell of breakfast lead me to the kitchen. Dad was cooking something delicious for a change, and Elliott was already halfway through his egg-and-bacon sandwich. I pulled up a chair and rested my chin on the counter. Before I could ask, Dad flopped me a sandwich on a plate and slid over a glass of chocolate milk.

"Morning, buddy! What's on the agenda for today?" Dad asked.

I took a bite of the sandwich and answered through a full mouth. "I dunno."

"No plans, huh?" Dad took a sip of his coffee. "Maybe you want to invite Grace over?"

Great. Now Dad knew about her, which meant I would have to deal with his heavy sarcasm for the rest of the year. The only thing I could do was accept the fact that both my parents knew and live with the consequences.

"Nah, that's okay," I mumbled. "Maybe later."

"Or maybe you want to hold her hand again!" Elliott laughed with his mouth open and spewed out some of his egg sandwich on the floor.

Dad stuck out his hand and high-fived Elliott.

I'd had enough and grabbed my plate to move to the living room, but Dad stopped me.

"We're just kidding, buddy," he apologized. "Stay here and eat with us for a while!"

"That's okay," I said.

Elliott was now trying to drown the bread stuck in his throat by gargling with milk.

"I think I'll enjoy my meal better over here," I added.

I sat down in our reclining chair and pulled the wooden lever to kick my feet up. Boy, it felt good to rest my foot.

Yesterday had been brutal, and today I really did need to rest if I wanted to get any better. I swiveled the chair to the front window to look outside at the howling wind. Sticks and twigs were bouncing across our gravel driveway, and all the trees were taking a bow toward the ground. Windy days in Colorado are almost like snow days in Minnesota or hurricane watches in Florida. When the wind comes out, you might as well stay inside, unless you want dust permanently stuck to your face.

I rocked in the chair and gobbled my sandwich and tried to relax my body as best I could. But as I ate, I watched a blue-and-orange blur spring up from behind the Monklings' fence and climb its way toward the sky. The blur paused for a second, and I realized what it was: a kite.

The driver of the kite didn't keep it in the air long; the wind quickly took control and forced the kite back to the ground, snapping the string it was on. The kite skidded across the rocks and landed right in front of our window, jamming itself inside some pine bushes.

I looked over at the Monklings' fence and saw Jenna's face peer up and search for her almost-destroyed kite. This was the perfect moment for me to finally talk to Jenna and maybe find out more about how Eric was feeling.

I grabbed my jacket, put on some flip-flops, and headed out the door. It was much windier than I had thought, and I had to take small steps so I wouldn't lose a flip-flop to the fast gusts of Colorado wind. I made my way to the bushes and grabbed the kite, which suddenly made it much harder to stand. The wind pushed and pulled and tried to take the kite back into the sky, but I stuffed part of it in my jacket and started walking toward the Monklings' house. Jenna met me halfway, and we sat under the giant willow tree that shared our property line.

"Thanks for grabbing it," Jenna said while trying to spit some hair out of her mouth. "I thought it was a goner."

"Yeah, no problem." I handed Jenna the kite, and she shoved it under her legs to keep it from flying away.

I flipped the front of my hair to keep it out of my eyes as the wind whipped another gust of leaves and dust. "Hey, Jenna, I wanted to say thanks again for that card. It really meant a lot to me."

Jenna kept her attention on the kite, which was trying to escape again. "I thought you might like it. It was the least I could do after what I did."

"What do you mean? I asked.

Jenna adjusted the kite so it was under her butt, then

folded her hands and wrapped them under her feet. "Well, I kinda made a wish . . ." Jenna said, staring at her feet.

"Okay, what kind of wish did you make?"

Jenna was hesitant, and I could tell whatever she was about to say was not going to come out easy.

"I'm really sorry, Matt. When you broke my collarbone, I made a wish that you would break yours too! It just came out!" Jenna's eyes welled up with tears, but none dropped.

"But I haven't broken a collarbone, Jenna! Everything is fine!" I chuckled a little to try to cheer her up, but I was actually trying to cheer *myself* up. I knew full well that Jenna's wish hadn't done anything to me. The Curse, however, was ruining my life.

"You've broken almost all of your toes, though, Matt. Isn't it obvious? Instead of a broken collarbone, you're going to break all your toes. My brothers told me all about the Curse!" Jenna stuck her head between her legs while the kite flapped and vibrated beneath her.

I don't know who had started the legend of the Curse, but it was now more real than ever. Saying I wasn't nervous would be a complete lie. So far, I'd broken five toes, and the Curse didn't seem to be getting any better as the year went on. In fact, it was getting worse.

"Jenna, look. Even if it is the Curse, I probably deserve it, okay? I ruined your entire summer! Don't worry about it. It's not your fault."

Jenna grabbed one of her pigtails and adjusted the

ribbon that held it together. "Are you sure? Do you really believe that?"

I didn't know what to believe, but to help Jenna, I said the words that I hoped would make her feel better: "Yep, you bet I do."

I wanted to ask her about Eric, but it didn't seem to fit the mood. Instead, I took the spool of string next to Jenna and playfully shoved her over, letting the wind catch the kite and skyrocket it into the air. Jenna giggled and grabbed onto the string with me, and we steered the kite together for a while, watching it dance with the leaves above our houses.

Eventually the wind won and sent the kite crashing to the ground, but neither Jenna nor I made an attempt to send it back up. We both seemed content and happy with how the windy conversation had gone.

"I need to go," Jenna said. "Can we hang out later? Maybe play some games I missed during summer vacation?"

"As long as you don't break any of my toes," I joked.

She smiled and waved goodbye, leaving me with the kite and the tangled string.

Spending time with Jenna had been what I'd needed. It had cleared up a lot of questions in my mind about her, but more importantly about the Curse.

It was real—no denying it. And my one chance to beat it was coming.

CHAPTER 21
THE TURKEY SHOOT-OUT

Truth be told, I don't remember much about the week after I talked to Jenna. Maybe I was too focused on the Turkey Shoot-Out the next weekend, or maybe my brain decided that whatever happened that week wasn't worth keeping. I do know one thing for sure, though: I didn't break any toes that week. *That* I would have remembered.

It was Saturday again, a week after our loss to Mountain View, and I found myself back on Summit Hill with my team for the Turkey Shoot-Out Tournament. It was an odd feeling coming back to the same field we'd just lost on a week before, but my sense of disappointment was shelved when I caught a glimpse of the first-place trophy underneath the winner's tent. It was taller than I was—a tower of gold beams and marble shelves that stole the attention from the mountains. I imagined myself holding it above my head, cheering with my team, and hoisting it in the air while we ran around the field. Winning the trophy didn't just mean a trip to Vegas, though—it meant breaking the Curse, and that was way more important to me than anything. I could have sat in front of that trophy all day, dreaming of breaking the Curse and traveling to Las Vegas, but I didn't, because dreaming doesn't get you anywhere.

Coach Cup must have been up all night. When he showed up to talk to us, his eyes were bloodshot red, and they blended right into his jersey. I'd like to think he was up all night strategizing for our next match, but I knew better than that. More than likely, Coach Cup was probably up all night watching football or practicing his insults for us in the mirror.

I thought for a second I should give him the benefit of the doubt since it was the biggest tournament of the year. But when he threw up all over his clipboard right before the first game, it was clear Coach Cup wouldn't be able to do much of anything.

Coach Reese didn't waste any time and barely gave the team time to react. He grabbed Coach Cup by the front collar of his jacket and marched him backward toward the bench next to the bleachers. Coach Cup didn't fight this at all. I don't think he had the energy or really knew what was going on. As soon as Coach Reese placed him down, Coach Cup fell to his side and went to sleep with one arm still resting on the top of the bench.

Coach Reese tried his best to give us a pep talk.

"Come on, guys! Coach Cup made his decision to skip

this game, but not you. You can all still win! Eagle Crest doesn't have a shot at beating us this time!"

It was a good effort, but as we walked onto the field, I could still feel the lack of energy in our team. I don't know why, either, because none of us were upset that Coach Cup was out of commission. Actually, it was what we had been waiting for—to have Coach Reese take over permanently and have a coach who actually cared about us for a change.

Anyway, it was like our team decided to lose before the ball was even kicked. By halftime, the score was 2–0, and Eagle Crest was already celebrating on the sideline while we all sat on the bench staring at our cleats.

I looked at my left foot, with the cotton that cushioned my toes puffing out the top. What was the point of stepping back on the field if we were already giving up? Just as I was feeling the dream of going to Las Vegas slowly slipping away, an Eagle Crest parent walked by.

"Enjoy the losers' bracket, maggots," laughed a small hobbit of a man as he jammed a sandwich in his mouth.

Before Coach Reese could get to him, Eric did.

"Go walk into traffic!" Eric yelled. The rest of the team backed him up and started throwing leftover orange peels at the man, who just kept laughing.

"Whatever you need to do to make yourselves feel better, boys! Haha!" He jogged back over to his side of the field and took his spot next to the team's water cooler.

I looked around, and every one of my teammates had the same expression. Every face was beet red, and I could feel the steam of hatred rising out of the center of our circle. Our goalie was clenching his fist, and Eric was tearing grass out of the ground like a dog about to charge.

Coach Reese chimed in. "Well, boys, if that doesn't get you pumped for the second half, I don't know what will."

Coach was right. We were all ticked, and our lack of energy had turned into a vengeful determination. Little did that Eagle Crest parent know his comment would cost his kid's team a chance to go to Vegas.

Coach Reese put Eric and me in as forward and uttered one line before we stepped onto the field: "Make 'em pay, boys! Make 'em pay!"

Oh, and we did make 'em pay. Whatever hatred Eric had for me disappeared, and for the next forty minutes, we dominated the game. Eric scored the first goal less than a minute into the second half. Seconds later, I nabbed the ball from a defender, then shot it into the upper-left corner of the goal, tying the game 2–2.

The rest of the game, Eric and I passed the ball back and forth, confusing each Eagle Crest player we encountered. With Eric and I on the same page, we were like ghosts. We did what we wanted, when we wanted, with that soccer ball, and no force could stop either of us, not even a broken toe. When the whistle finally blew at the end of the game, the score was Montrose Mountaineers: 7, Eagle Crest: 2. Eagle Crest seemed somewhat happy that their embarrassment in front of the crowd was over.

Eric made sure to trot over to their water cooler, where the short, hobbit-like man sat dumbfounded in his seat.

"Oh, hey! Enjoy the loser's bracket, jerk," Eric muttered. Then he ran over and put his arm over me, and we celebrated with the rest of the team. Even if it lasted only a short time, for the moment, Eric and I were friends again.

Coach Reese shared in the joy with the rest of the team. "That . . . that was incredible! Team, way to persevere! Okay, go get some lunch and be back here at 3:00. I want you all here a little early for the next game. We are only one win away from Vegas, boys!"

The team let out a final cheer and then split up to find their families for lunch. My family and I stayed on Summit Hill and had a picnic together near the pond while everyone else left for town. For a little while, we were the only ones up there, besides the referees guarding the trophy and Coach Cup passed out on the bench.

I gobbled up some tuna salad and was about to have a

slice of cake Mom had brought from home when Elliott cut me off.

"So, Matt, do you think the Curse will get you on the soccer field?" he asked.

He was dead serious, but Mom and Dad didn't pick up on it. They just rolled their eyes and continued to eat.

I leaned in close to Elliott to tell him my plan. "Nah, I don't think it will," I whispered. "In fact, I think if I win today, the Curse will disappear!"

Elliott's eyes grew wide, and I explained to him what I had read in English class about the Egyptians.

"Whoa, that's cool stuff," Elliott said and grabbed his slice of cake from the basket. "Good luck. You're gonna need it."

"I know. At least I can enjoy this cake. Did you try it? It's amazing!"

"No. Really?" Elliott asked and leaned his face toward the plate.

He didn't get to enjoy a single bit, though, because when he lifted his plate to take a bite, I pushed it up right into his face. I laughed as he wiped frosting off.

"Hey! What did you do that for?!" he yelled.

I could tell by the look on Mom's face I was in trouble, but it was worth it.

"That's what you get for wasting the leftover mashed potatoes in my ice bucket last month," I said.

Three o'clock rolled around quicker than I thought it would, and it wasn't enough time for my toes to stop beating in pain from the last game. I took out the last of my cotton ball supply and stuffed my cleat one last time. My toes just had to make it through one last game, just one, and then they could rest.

All my teammates showed up on time, and Coach spent the next hour talking about our opponents, the Durango Dust Devils. They were undefeated that season and had a reputation for playing cheap. Even their parents had a legacy of being rowdy fans, yelling and jeering comments that Mom would ground me for if I said.

We had some extra support in the stands this time, though. Grace had organized a group of kids from school to come, and they showed up to the game with their faces painted and holding up giant signs like "Go, Montrose!" and "Matt's my hero!" Henry and John came too but they sat away from Grace. I think they were scared of her yelling, "Crush 'em, Montrose! CRUSH 'EM!" She can be a bit over the top sometimes . . .

With our team warm-up complete, I took my spot on the field. I stretched and touched my toes one last time for good luck, then looked up to let the sun warm my face before the ref placed the ball on the ground. It was my last chance to soak in the moment of being in the finals, because as soon as the ref started the game, the next ninety minutes would give me no rest.

Durango started with the ball and pushed hard up our side of the field. They were a fast team and moved together in one force, which caught our team off guard. We battled in the backfield, and our defenders managed to deflect their first shot away from the goal. I chased after it, but my speed wasn't an advantage. A Durango Dust Devil met me at the ball, and we jostled for it.

We bumped and pushed as we fought for the ball. Just as I managed to win and take a stride in the other direction toward their goal, the Durango player grabbed my shorts and yanked them downward, causing me to lose focus on the game and snatch my shorts before they fell down. Before I could throw my arms up in the air to complain, the Devil shot the ball, and it whizzed past our goalie into the net. Dust Devils: 1, Mountaineers: 0.

"Hey, kid! Make sure your pants don't fall down! Maybe you need a smaller size!" shouted some lady from the stands.

I tried to ignore her, but she kept going.

"Yeah, I'm talking to you! Go shop in the baby aisle and get yourself a nice pair of diapers!"

What kind of mother yells something like that at a kids' soccer game? She kept repeating herself until I was out of earshot, but I knew as soon as I got close to her again, I'd be in for another royal treatment of insults. The only way to get her to quit it was to score a goal—or punch her in the mouth. Since I couldn't punch her, I set out to do the next best thing: score.

The ref blew the whistle, and I passed the ball to Eric, who blew past a defender and made his way down the sideline. Eric was greeted by a giant "Booooo!" from the stands as he sprinted by, but he didn't care. Eric heel-kicked the ball to Tyler, our center, who lined up for a shot. I raced down to the far side of the goal and called for him, but Tyler had already connected and the ball was sailing through the air. The goalie threw his hands up in the air for the save, but I jumped up at the last second and ricocheted the ball off my head and into the goal. Mountaineers: 1, Dust Devils: 1.

My goal silenced the Dust Devils parents, who sat back down and muttered among themselves.

Coach Reese handed out water as we caught our breath before the next half. "Way to go out there, boys! Keep passing the ball to move it forward, and try to draw attention to their midfielders and . . ."

Eric leaned over to me while Coach continued his half-time speech. "Nice goal, Matt. Think you can do another?"

"I got kinda lucky with that one, but I'll try. Nice footwork out there, by the way," I complimented.

He nodded and turned his attention back to Coach. He was being friendlier, but it was still not like how things used to be.

"And just give it 110 percent out there!" Coach ended. "Mountaineers on three! One, two . . ."

"MOUNTAINEERS!" our fans whooped. I looked up to see Grace, my family, Henry, John, and Eric's family cheering from the stands. This was *our* moment, and the Curse was going to be broken in the process.

Both sides of the bleachers cheered as we battled with the Dust Devils during the second half. As loud as they were, the screaming fans weren't doing either team much good. Neither team could get a shot toward the goal, and it seemed we were going to be deadlocked until one team passed out from exhaustion. Even the player who had tried to pull my shorts down was drained, and he could barely run back and forth when the ball transitioned from one team to the other. The game was a pinball machine, and neither team could get control.

There are some moments in life, good and bad, that go in slow motion. You know what I'm talking about. It's like you're part of the movie, but you have an outside view of everything going on. Your mind works three times faster, but your body mechanics are stuck in one slow speed, and every smell and every sense are raised to a superhero level. The end of the game with the Dust Devils was like that. It was the longest slow-motion movie I would ever be a part of.

With two minutes to go before the game was over, Coach Reese pulled Eric and me and put two of our teammates in. I couldn't argue with his decision. Eric and I were dead tired, and we were worthless to our team on the field. All I could do now was sit and watch my team from the bench, and that's when everything slowed down.

My stomach knotted, and a rock formed in my throat so large I had to push my chest with my hands to make myself breathe in. Our goalie threw the ball to a defender, who dribbled the ball up to midfield and passed to Tyler.

One minute left.

Tyler dodged an attack from a monstrous-looking Devil and kept the ball to himself to try to position for a shot.

Thirty seconds left.

Tyler flipped the ball over his head around the last Devil defender and took two final steps.

Fifteen seconds.

"Shoot the ball, Tyler! Shoot it!" Coach Reese was on the top of the bench screaming at the top of his lungs, his hands cupping his mouth.

Tyler drew his leg forward to strike and blasted the ball.

Ten seconds.

The goalie dived, hands stretched as far as they could go. The ball smacked the white goalie gloves, then, with some encouragement from the crowd, snail-rolled past the white line and into the net. Mountaineers: 2, Dust Devils: 1. Game over!

The slow motion suddenly went to fast-forward, and the next five minutes were a blur of celebration and hugs. The Dust Devils dropped to the ground and covered their faces, but the Mountaineers crowd stormed the field and swarmed Tyler. Our team joined hands and jumped into the crowd of people, finally finding Tyler and congratulating him on the best minute of soccer I'd ever seen anyone play. I caught a glimpse of Coach Cup, still snoozing on the bench. He'd missed it all.

The trophy was handed to Coach Reese, who held it low so the entire team could touch it. It was a surreal feeling. We'd won, and we would get to play in Las Vegas during the summer. The camp, practices, running through the pain of broken toes had paid off, and boy, had it been worth it. Best of all, I had won something big—something so big it must have broken the Curse.

A photographer from the Montrose paper approached

us for our championship picture. I raised the trophy high into the air as the bulb of the camera flashed over and over. It was one of the greatest moments of my life.

CHAPTER 22
THE MAGIC 8 BALL

It's weird how one event can change your entire reputation in middle school. If you were popular but were caught playing in a sandbox like a little kid, you would lose friends quicker than sweaters go to the clearance section in May. On the flip side, you could be an outcast and suddenly become popular because you'd bought a trendy pair of jeans. I definitely hadn't been part of the popular clique when I got to Centennial Middle School. The Curse made sure of that.

But that changed when our team won the soccer tournament. I received superstar status overnight. It was now November, only a few days after the soccer tournament, and kids I didn't even know came up to me and told me what a great game it had been.

"Hey, Sprouts! Sweet game, man!" said Random Kid Number One.

"Dude, that was awesome! You get to go to Vegas?" yelled Random Kid Number Two.

In the midst of my heroic soccer fame, they had all seemed to forget about the Curse, and that change had plenty of benefits. The teachers were nicer, seventh graders said hi to me in the hall, and Grace and I were liking each other more and more, which a few months ago I didn't think would be possible. What a curveball!

"*My* boyfriend scored one of the final goals, and he is going to take me to Las Vegas with him!" I caught her bragging to a group of seventh-grade girls outside our lockers the next week.

Only part of what she said was true: I wasn't taking Grace to Vegas. Just the thought of going on a vacation with her seemed stressful. Plus, I didn't have the money to take her. I let her have the moment, though. It felt good to be liked by everyone for a change, and Grace was obviously enjoying the attention too, so I didn't want to take it away from her. The best part of the entire situation, though? I had broken the Curse. No more broken toes would be in my future. Period.

The only person the win didn't change—and you probably guessed it—was Mrs. Klinkle. We all thought Mrs. Grubbles would have returned to teach by now, but we weren't that lucky. She was still healing, so we were still stuck with Mrs. Klinkle.

"Ah, and here comes Mr. Popular, Matt Sprouts. Are you going to participate today, or are you still basking in the glory of your soccer trophy?" she announced one day when I entered class.

What could I say to something like that? I just took my seat and opened my book to our last reading to try to diffuse the situation, but that didn't work. She kept pestering me.

"I see. No response? Too popular to have a conversation with a lowly teacher like myself, Mr. Sprouts?" The sarcasm in her voice reminded me a lot of Dad's when he was angry. "Well, then, how about you begin reading for us, starting on page 130?"

And that's how English class went for the rest of November. I was Mrs. Klinkle's pin cushion, and no matter how hard I tried, how little I talked, or how much I participated, she always found something wrong with what I did or didn't do. Even Grace, with her mighty groveling skills, couldn't protect me. It was just Mrs. Klinkle and me, boxing it out each and every day.

On the bright side, my toes were healing up. Playing soccer on two broken toes had definitely slowed the healing process, but by the end of November they looked normal next to each other, and I didn't need cotton to cushion them anymore—especially since the Curse was now broken.

The end of November also brought something else. It was almost winter, and the snow was starting to fall in the mountains—and lightly in Montrose. It's funny how easily the snow transforms the landscape into a completely different world too. My backyard became a blanket of white, and sometimes I thought the mountains, with their newly covered tops, were clouds. The transition of seasons helped school go by faster, and winter break came up quicker than I could have hoped. Good thing, because I needed a break from Mrs. Klinkle.

Finally, in mid-December, school was out, and all I could focus on was Christmas. At my house, Christmas is a big tradition, and we always jam-pack the day with presents, snowshoeing, and a dinner so big it lasts us most of winter break. Yeah, you could say Christmas is my favorite time of the year in the Sprouts house.

It was going to be a great one too, because Grace was coming over for Christmas Eve lunch with my family.

Elliott answered the door before I could get there. "Maaaaaaatt! Your girlfriend is here!"

I rounded the corner to the front door and helped Grace take off her coat, but Elliott stuck around to ask her a few pressing questions.

"How come you're so short?" Elliott asked. He stood next to Grace and compared heights. "I'm younger and almost taller than you!" He wasn't saying it to be mean; I think he just wondered why a girl in middle school was as short as him.

I answered for Grace. "Actually, Elliott, she's getting taller. I've noticed."

It was true. Grace had been slowly growing over the past few months. The only reason I had caught on to her growth spurt was from the surprise hugs she gave me in the middle of class (which were the best parts of my day). Her head wasn't hitting my belly button anymore—it was almost hitting my chin.

Grace smiled, and we went to the living room and watched Mom prepare lunch. Mom was an amazing dance teacher, but watching her in the kitchen was like watching a professional football player throw a touchdown pass or a math genius solve a puzzle. Cooking was a masterpiece that only Mom could do well. Plus, sitting near the kitchen meant Grace and I could lick all the mixing spoons from the cookie dough, but that meant Mom got to talk to Grace. This could be a disaster. Who knew what odd or embarrassing things Mom would say or ask?

"So, Grace," Mom said as she scooped us a chunk of cookie dough. "What kind of stuff do you like to do?"

It was like Grace was waiting for the question, and she practically shouted. "Oh my gosh, I absolutely *love* building stuff. I build things all the time!"

"Really?" Mom said. "Like what?"

I listened, curious. Grace never told me she liked building, but I guess I never asked either.

"You name it!" Grace exclaimed. "I've built napkin holders and bird houses, but my favorite so far was our kitchen table."

"You built a table?"

"Well, yeah!" Grace giggled. "My mom is a woodworker, and we make all sorts of things together in the shop."

"You know," Mom said while handing Grace another dip of cookie dough, "I do need some new set pieces built for the dance recital this year. Would you and your mom be interested in designing something?"

Grace practically exploded. "Oh wow! Yes! That would be great! I've never made something for a stage before!"

I licked the dough off the spoon while Mom and Grace continued to talk about their design ideas. And the more I listened to Grace, the more I wanted to know! I once heard that people are full of surprises, but I don't think that's true. I think you just have to ask more questions— that's all.

So I sat and tried to think about what other questions I should start asking Grace to get to know her better, but I was interrupted. Elliott was beginning his early Christmas present assault on Dad, which was a yearly ritual.

"Can I just open one? Puuh-lease?! Just one, that's it," he begged.

Dad moved between the Christmas tree and Elliott. "Elliott, we go over this every year. Just wait till tomorrow."

"Maaannnnnn! Why can't we do what I want to do?! Just one. Please, Dad, I'm begging you!"

Dad gave up easier than I thought. "Fine, but I get to pick the present for you and Matt. I'll be right back."

Elliott pumped his fists in the air, and Grace and I got down on the floor with him to wait for my present. Dad had never given in to Elliott before, so I guessed whatever he was about to give us was going to be either a joke or something really spectacular.

Dad carefully brought in a cardboard box, and Mom took a break from the kitchen and joined us on the carpet in front of the tree. Whatever the gift was, it wasn't even wrapped. As Dad placed it down on the floor, Nala ran in from behind the couch and stuck her nose in the box.

"Move your head, Nala! Get out of the way!" Elliott grabbed Nala and gently pulled her back. "Matt, move the box closer so I can see it!"

Dad slowly pushed the box toward us, and Elliott, Grace, and I leaned forward to view the first Christmas present of the year. Inside, curled up in a tight fuzzy ball, was a bright-orange tabby kitten.

"Oh, he is so cute I can hardly stand it!" Mom exclaimed as she picked up our sleeping new pet. "This was so hard to keep a secret from you boys."

"Seriously," Dad added. "I'm more of a dog person, but this little one is adorable."

"I've been asking for a kitten for forever!" Elliott screamed. "You finally found one! Let me see 'em!" Mom softly handed the kitten to Elliott, who immediately pressed him against his face. "He's so soft!"

The kitten woke at the sound of Elliott's excitement and gave a big yawn for everyone to see.

"What a cutie!" Grace started to point out, but I was too distracted by the kitten's mouth.

"Hey, Dad," I said, "why doesn't this cat have any teeth?" Mom and Elliott opened the kitten's mouth to make sure I wasn't lying.

"About that," Dad started to explain. "I guess he might not have any. The veterinarian at the shelter said it's odd he doesn't have any yet, since he is three months old already."

"How is he supposed to chew his food, Dad? With his gums?" Elliott asked.

"I guess so," Dad laughed. "Maybe we should call him Gummers."

My family looked at one another and then at Grace for approval. No one seemed to disagree with Dad's suggestion. It was a goofy name, but he *was* a goofy cat. I took Gummers from Elliott and held him at my chest, and he started purring right away.

"Looks like he's found a friend!" Grace squealed.

I held Gummers at the dinner table while we ate Mom's delicious cranberry turkey lunch. It was a gourmet feast, and I ate until my stomach was bloated. When we were all finished, Mom cleared the table while Elliott quizzed Dad about what other presents might be under the tree. With everyone distracted, Grace said it was time for her to leave and get home to her own family.

I handed Gummers off to Elliott, and Grace took my hand and led me to the front door, where she moved her jacket and revealed a small box wrapped in yellow paper.

"This is for you," Grace said, handing the present to me.

I cut the red ribbon with my fingernail and removed the yellow wrapping. I pulled out a black orb, about the size of a baseball. I had no idea what it was, and Grace picked up on my confusion.

"It's a Magic 8 Ball. It helps you answer tough questions. Here, let me show you," she explained. She rolled the ball over in my hands to expose a clear, circular window. "Will Matt give me a kiss tonight?" she asked, then shook the ball. We both gazed at the window, and slowly words began to appear on a triangular pad. When the liquid around the words disappeared, the triangle read, ***"YES."***

A kiss? I mean, I wanted to. *But how do you even do a kiss? Do you press your face against their face? How do you breathe?! Do I lean in first, or do I wait? Do I close my eyes? How will I know where I am going? Are there instructions I can read to—* And then it was happening. My first kiss. I don't know how it happened. One minute I was panicking, and the next moment Grace and I were sharing our first kiss. It sent a tingly sensation across the entire left side of my check, which reminded me of fall days, when the sun peeks out from behind the clouds for just enough time to warm your face from the cool air.

"GROSS!" Elliott yelled. His head was peeking around the corner of the next room, and just like that my first kiss was over. Grace and I looked at each other, then at Elliott (who was covering his mouth like he was sick), and laughed.

"Merry Christmas, Matt," Grace giggled, then grabbed her coat and walked out the door, got in the car with her parents, and drove away.

I went and sat back down with my brother and Dad and started shuffling around more presents. Grace's kiss had put me in a spell, and all I could do was replay the moment over and over in my head while I held onto the magic eight ball.

"A Magic 8 Ball!" Elliott noticed. "Does it work?"

That was a complicated question. I mean, the ball had known that Grace and I would kiss, so what else did it know?

"I'm not sure," I said. "Why don't you try it?"

I let the ball roll out of my hand and across the table to

Elliott, who was already starting to ask the Magic 8 Ball a question. "Oh, mighty Magic 8 Ball, will my brother break any more toes?" He shook it hard, and I could hear the triangle word pad tinging the walls of the orb.

Elliott set it down on the table so everyone could see. The liquid stared to fade, and I muttered to myself the four-letter word that appeared: **SOON**. The familiar cold nothingness crept onto my shoulders once again, and I found myself covering my mouth to keep from chattering my teeth.

The Magic 8 Ball was a toy—a cheap manufactured piece of plastic. But it scared me. The thought of another broken toe settled in my stomach, and it made me want to vomit. The cold nothingness didn't help, either.

"'Soon'? Ha! Stinks to be you, Matt! I wonder what toe you'll break next. I guess the Curse is still going!" Elliott laughed heartily.

Dad could see the concern in my face. "Oh, those things are just jokes, Matt. They're a bunch of hooey. You'll be fine."

But I wasn't fine. I wanted to believe him, but I couldn't. Winning the Turkey Shoot-Out, I just assumed I'd beaten the Curse, but I'd never proved it. The possibility that the Curse was still alive was haunting, and I could sense another broken toe coming my way. How would it happen? I didn't know. I just knew it would happen—soon.

CHAPTER 23
TOES SIX AND SEVEN

Humans were not designed to leave the ground, period. Gravity (you know, Earth trying to pull you down to the ground) is there for a reason, and it's a sign that people are not built to fly or go higher than they can jump with two feet. I mean, think about it. If we were supposed to fly, we'd have insect wings or maybe giant feathers. Airplanes, pogo sticks, and gliders are just distractions from reality. They make us forget that leaving the ground for any reason is a big mistake.

Be grateful that I'm sharing this information, because I learned it too late and paid a hefty price. You see, if I'd known this before Christmas Day, I could have saved myself an embarrassing moment, expensive crutches, and some broken toes.

Christmas morning for a lot of kids meant opening presents and playing with them alone in their room. This was not the case in my family. We did things a little differently and actually spent some time together. Elliott and I teamed up to wake Mom and Dad at 5:30 sharp Christmas morning.

"Get up! It's Christmas!" Elliott screamed and ran into our parents' room.

I followed in after him and jumped on the bed. You would think our parents would scream in shock, but they were used to it. They rubbed their eyes, smiled at us, put on their robes, and followed us out the door.

We all opened presents until 6:30 a.m., then we ate a large egg bake Mom had prepared the night before. By 7:30 a.m., the entire Sprouts family was packed in the car to leave for the mountains. To do what, you ask? Simple: use our ski passes we got from Mom and Dad for working for the Klinkles! A family ski trip! Wahoo!

So at exactly 7:30 Christmas morning, all four of us crammed in the car with the snowboards strapped to the top, heading to Telluride for a day full of high-mountain skiing adventures. Mom and Dad sipped their coffee and talked about work while we made our way through the icy mountain range, but I didn't have anyone to talk with. Elliott was too busy speaking to the Magic 8 Ball he had stolen from my room.

"Will I be a millionaire someday?" Elliott asked, shaking the ball.

"NO," read the ball.

"Will I be a billionaire someday?" he asked.

"NO," read the ball.

Elliott would not give up. "Will I be a bazillion-trillion-aire someday, then?!"

"TRY AGAIN LATER," read the ball.

"Did you see that, Matt?! Did you? It said I'm going to be a bazillion-trillionaire someday!" Elliott boasted. He did a small fist pump in the air and slapped his knee. I couldn't believe he actually had faith in that thing.

I rolled my eyes. "Great, Elliott," I said sarcastically. "Enjoy your fortune."

Elliott asked the Magic 8 Ball questions all the way to Telluride. By the end of the ride, I wanted to take the ball and huck it into the icy river, where it would never be seen again. The only thing the ball did was scare me, and I didn't want to think about what it had said about the Curse anymore. All I wanted was to snowboard and forget the Curse.

We parked in Mountain Village, a resort of condos in the middle of the mountain that reminded me a lot of Dr. Seuss buildings. They were oddly shaped, and the colors didn't quite match, like lime green and dark orange. The buildings were filled with rich executives, movie stars, and professional athletes. I think they live in Telluride to hide away from the public and magazine photographers. It's impossible to recognize anyone in snow gear. That's what I think.

Elliott, Mom, Dad, and I strapped on our snowboards and got in line for the first lift. We could see the entire mountain slope with people cutting their way through the snow and powder kicking up in their faces. I couldn't wait to get down there, and Elliot couldn't either. He'd already spied his favorite place: Jump Park.

Jump Park is just what it sounds like—lots of jumps. It's a series of large snow mounds you can launch yourself off of, and if you're really good, you can land on metal pipes and grind on top of the snow. I avoid the area because people who hang out there are weird. They all have crusty hair and smell like old wet clothes.

"Ah, man! I'm going there first! Do you see that guy? He's gonna get so high!" Elliott pointed.

I watched as a man approached a mound of snow. He tucked his body close to the snowboard and launched himself high into the air. Elliott was mystified.

"Sweet! I love Jump Park! Want to come with me, Matt?!" he asked.

"Uh, sure. Why not? I'd love to see you wipe out," I said jokingly. It made me remember the last time we'd gone snowboarding, when Elliott had fallen and gotten snow up his nose.

"Your mom and I are going to a more relaxing run. You boys be safe," Dad mentioned as I kept snickering from the memory of Elliott. "We'll see you both soon."

We waved bye to our parents. Our boards flapped the

powdered slope as we got off the lift. I followed Elliott through the snow-dusted pines to the entrance of Jump Park, and we stopped right next to the park warning sign:

WARNING!

EXPERIENCED RIDERS ONLY

After I finished reading, the cold nothingness snuck inside my jacket and filled my lungs. It was the Curse. A warning, maybe, but it was the Curse. I knew *the feeling* and knew what it meant.

I debated unstrapping my board, but Elliott took off his goggles and got my attention.

"Matt! Check this out. I'm gonna hit that small jump on the side over there and land on that rail!"

Elliott snapped his goggles back in place and aimed his board at the jump. I'm sure he thought his cocky attitude would help, but it didn't. When he reached the top of the jump, his board caught the ground, and he tumbled across the top of the snow. The only "air time" he would be able to brag about was when his body had bounced during the fall.

A group of hippie snowboarders were sitting nearby on the hill and saw the whole thing. "Yo, dude! Nice wipeout!" said a guy wearing jean overalls and a stained jacket. His buddies were laughing, so I threw out a joke too.

"Wow, Elliott! That was incredible! Could you teach me how to do that?" I teased.

Elliott's snow-filled helmet appeared from the other side of the jump, and he brushed off his face. "Haha. Real funny, Matt. Let's see you try it, then—or are you too chicken?"

Usually I'd pass, but the thought of landing the jump and rubbing it in Elliott's face sounded too good. "Move over," I huffed. "Watch and learn."

I let go of the fence and let my board guide me through the snow to the front of the jump. I crouched low to gain speed and put my arms out for balance. If I was going to do the jump, I was gonna do it big and really impress Elliott.

The snowbank inclined, and I extended my legs to catch sight of the landing. Then my heart sank. As my board left the ground from the top of the jump, I decided I didn't want to do it anymore. I didn't want to jump. I didn't want to leave the ground. But it was too late. The landing was far away, and I was going too fast and too high. I panicked in midair, and my arms flailed violently to try to stay balanced. My head led my body as I sailed through the cold air. Gravity then took control and brought me back to earth. If I would have worn a red cape, I bet people would have mistaken me for a flying superhero.

My hands broke the ground first to try to stop the rest of me from hitting, but my arms gave way and my face smashed the snow. My board followed and brought the rest of my body over my head, and I began somersaulting down Jump Park. I probably could have rolled to the bottom of the hill where Mom and Dad would have comforted me, but the Curse had planned something much worse.

My board snagged a baby spruce tree, jamming my left foot deep into the snow, bringing me to a complete stop. My body pulsed, and I could hear my heartbeat in the back of my head. I was numb and didn't move a muscle. For all I knew, my arms could have fallen off and a coyote could have taken them away.

"Bro? Hey, dude . . . Ha! You okay?" said a voice. "That was a sick tumble."

Two hands grabbed my legs and flipped me to my back, and I felt my entire body come back to life. I kept my eyes closed and took a few deep breaths.

"That baby tree wrecked you hard, man! Almost as bad as that jump," said the voice. Two hands unclipped my boots from the board, and I heard a crunch noise as the hands stuck the board in the snow. My eyes opened to get a look at my helper. It was the hippie guy, the one with the overalls and jacket. He flipped his long brown hair back, then sat down on top of his board.

"I'm Dylan, the Jump Park ski patrol officer," he said. "Anything hurt, dude?"

"My ankle or my foot. I can't tell," I responded.

"All right, man! Let's check it!" He untied the left boot and wiggled it off as I winced in pain. "These socks gotta go too," he said and took out a pair of scissors and cut the wool sock down the side. I closed my eyes just in case he missed and got my skin.

"Oh man. That's broken for sure, dude. Yeah, definitely

broken. Maybe the ones next to it too," Dylan said, almost happily, as he rotated my foot.

I knew right then he wasn't talking about my ankle. I opened my eyes and saw that my biggest toe (the other Big Bubba) was sideways, and the one next to it was swollen. Broken. Ugh.

Dylan held up his walkie-talkie and called in a request: "We're gonna need to mummify this dude down the mountain. Bring it in."

"Mummify?" I asked.

"You'll see. I'm surprised you're not cryin'. Your toe is almost upside down, man!"

I stayed silent. It hurt, but after five broken-toe experiences, I was getting used to dealing with the pain. I shut my eyes and waited to get "mummified."

Another ski patrol officer with a snowmobile showed up towing an orange sled. He pulled up next to us and put out his cigarette in the snow. They both rolled me into the sled and tied me down with Velcro straps and pulled a large yellow sheet over my body. The only thing left showing was my head. I looked like an ancient Egyptian mummy.

It made me think of the moment in English class when I'd thought I could defeat the Curse. Mrs. Klinkle had made me read that statement on Egyptian curses, about how they could be defeated after overcoming an enemy or challenge. Clearly, this was the Curse's way of mocking me—sending me down the mountain in a yellow sled.

Dylan towed me down the mountain to the patrol center, where Elliott, Mom, and Dad were already waiting for me.

"I went to tell Dad when I saw ski patrol," Elliott said. "Sorry I left you."

I tried to nod, but my head was still strapped in the sled. Dylan and his buddy unstrapped and lifted me into a wheelchair. Dad took the handles and followed Dylan through the front doors and past the front desk into a small white room with a wooden table. A poster hung from the wall:

> **IT'S GONNA HURT. BUT IT'LL FEEL BETTER LATER.**

Not a very welcoming sign.

Dad hoisted me onto the wooden table. It had visible nails poking out the side, and it rocked unsteadily as I shifted my weight. Dylan bent down and put his dry, cracked hands on my foot. "You may want to hold on to something, dude. This is gonna hurt," he advised.

"Wait. What's going to hurt?" I asked.

Too late. Dylan grabbed hold of my big toe and twisted it violently. I heard a small cracking noise, and I screamed out a word I'd heard Coach Cup yell before.

"Matthew Sprouts! We do not use that type of language in this family!" Mom lectured.

Was she serious?! I sat with my mouth open, looking at her in disbelief. I'd love to see her try not to cuss when someone yanked on one of *her* broken bones.

"I had to reset the bone of the big toe. It was out of whack," Dylan said.

"Gee, thanks," I moaned and bit my lip to distract my mind from the pulsing torment of swirling pain that surrounded my big toe and the one next to it.

Dylan pulled Dad aside and handed him some papers while he went into a back room. He returned holding a pair of old crutches that had red washcloths duct-taped to the top.

Dad motioned that it was time to go, so I hopped up onto one foot and let the crutches bear my weight. They felt unsteady, and I was sure I could have built better crutches with twigs from my backyard.

Dad led us to a coffee shop just a little way from the ski lift and ordered hot chocolate for all of us. We found a booth in the back and snuggled in together and waited for our order.

"I don't know how you managed to do it, Matt. I'm stumped," Dad said, shaking his head. "Your broken toes are costing me a fortune."

Elliott felt like he knew the solution. "It's all right, Dad. The Magic 8 Ball said I'm going be a bazillion-trillionaire someday. I can pay for it," he said proudly.

Dad chuckled. "As long as Matt is okay."

I let my head fall onto Mom's shoulder, and she stroked my hair with the back of her hand. Breaking toes and taping them was one thing, but having crutches was a new game I wasn't prepared for.

"How many broken toes does that make for you now, Matt?" Mom asked. "Five?"

"Counting these today? Seven," I moaned.

"Yep! Only three more to go!" Elliott said joyfully.

"What do you mean, El, 'three more to go'?" Mom questioned again.

"Matt has to break three more toes to be even with Jenna, Mom. Then the Curse will be over. It's fair."

"Life doesn't work that way," she corrected.

"How does it work, then?" Elliott asked, his face serious. "Does he need to break a leg too?"

Everyone at the table laughed except me, and I suddenly felt alone. Of course they could laugh, because none of them had to worry. I had the Curse. It was *me* who had to bear the weight of wondering whether I'd break another toe and *me* who had to worry whether I was finally even with Jenna. My anger could have boiled my hot chocolate.

Winning the Turkey Shoot-Out hadn't ended the Curse. It had just postponed it.

CHAPTER 24
BACK TO REALITY

I'd like to tell you my Christmas vacation got better after breaking toes six and seven, but it didn't. The next three weeks were spent either sitting on the couch with Gummers and Nala or lying in bed playing video games while my family enjoyed the outdoors. Every kid thinks that playing video games all day is awesome, but try playing them for three weeks straight and then see how you feel. My eyes caved in from being in the dark, and my stomach hurt from all the chocolate I ate. Some days, my brain even lost touch with reality, and I'd mix up the real world with the fantasy from video games.

The worst came the last week when I was lying on the living room couch.

"Here you go, buddy. Try one of these. They're great!" Dad said and threw me a green apple. At the time, though, it didn't look like an apple to me.

I screamed in a high-pitched "Ahhhhh!" and dived off the couch. I made sure to grab a pillow to protect myself from the explosion.

"What on earth is wrong with you?" Dad laughed. "Did you think the apple would hurt you?"

Apple? Did he mean a dangerous grenade able to blow my head off? Because that is exactly what I had seen. I lifted the pillow from my head and saw the apple lying next to the chair. There was no grenade—and nothing to be scared of. Being trapped inside the house with only video games was slowing driving me nuts.

Luckily—or unluckily—for me, whichever way you wanted to look at it, school started up again midway through

January. I still had the crutches, but I was getting used to them, at least a little. I could balance on them both pretty good, and they gave me a brand new place to display my favorite hockey stickers.

The first day back at school, Mom dropped me off earlier than usual so I could have some extra time to make my way around. Grace, like always, was waiting for me at the front of the building, but she looked a lot different. She'd been in Florida for the past month, and although we talked most evenings on the phone, it didn't take away from the fact that I missed her. She appeared taller (how she grew so fast, I'll never know), but she was also tanner, which was a completely different look from her usual pale skin.

When she saw the crutches, she dropped her books and ran toward me.

"Oh no! You didn't tell me you got crutches too!" she said. "I thought it would just be a boot again!"

"I try not to think about them, which is probably why I didn't mention it," I said. "Can you help carry my books?"

Grace held my things, and I told her the details of the Christmas Day crash as we walked to our lockers. She shook her head in disbelief and blamed the entire situation on the hippie snowboarder, and I smiled. That's one thing I was beginning to love about Grace: she was always on my side, no matter what the story was.

When we got to English class, my classmates were lined up outside the door.

"What's going on?" Grace asked one of her friends.

"NEXT!" a voice crackled from inside the room.

"We're getting a new seating chart," the girl responded and stepped into the classroom.

It made sense to me. Since Mrs. Klinkle was gone now after teaching two spine-chilling months as a sub for Mrs. Grubbles, Mrs. Grubbles probably wanted to start fresh with a new seating chart.

"NEXT!" Mrs. Grubbles yelled from the room. She sounded grumpy and a lot like someone else I knew . . . I just couldn't put my finger on whom. I entered the room to get my new seat, and then I understood why I'd recognized the voice—it was Mrs. Klinkle.

"Mr. Sprouts, glad you could make it back. How about you sit right here, so I can keep an eye on you," she said and pointed to the chair closest to her desk.

I clicked down the aisle and sat in front of Mrs. Klinkle,

252 MATT SPROUTS AND THE CURSE OF THE TEN BROKEN TOES

who was still wearing the same purple outfit as before. I guess it's hard to buy new clothes for yourself when all you get in your stocking for Christmas is coal.

Mrs. Klinkle ignored everyone else still standing at the door and started writing on the board. The fastest kids got to the back seats first, and the others had to take their place in my row, which I appropriately named "The Last Place on Earth," because it was the last place on earth I'd want to be—smack-dab in front of Mrs. Klinkle.

"As some of you now know, I am the new permanent English teacher. Mrs. Grubbles will not be coming back to Centennial Middle School this year," Mrs. Klinkle announced.

There was a small gasp among the class, and I'm pretty sure I heard a few bad words muttered between the desks.

"Now, things will be a little different starting today," Mrs. Klinkle continued. "I have a new project for you."

A collective groan rose in the room.

Mrs. Klinkle sent us out of class with a stack of papers so high it could have fueled our family's fireplace all winter. Thankfully, Grace took my stack to my locker, and I headed off to woodshop, thinking about how miserable my life would be for the next month, trying to finish Mrs. Klinkle's assignments.

I was running late too. My armpits were chafing from the washcloths on the crutches, and I had to stop once in the hallway before my pits spontaneously exploded from the rubbing. By the time I got to woodshop, there was only one seat left, and it was next to Eric.

I thought things would change with him after the Turkey Shoot-Out win, but they didn't. We didn't talk on the phone or even make an attempt to hang out with each other. It was like we were never friends in the first place, and that hurt. It hurt a lot.

I sat down on the stool and leaned my crutches against the desk, but Eric didn't say anything. He stayed silent through the entire class. Even when the teacher told us to work with our partner on a measuring lab, Eric asked for another ruler and did it on his own. What a great reintroduction to school after winter break: Mrs. Klinkle's long, boring assignment and a friend who still wouldn't talk to me. Fabulous. Just fabulous.

The end of the day finally came, and I made my way to the bus pickup. Mom's new dance classes overlapped with the end of the school day, which meant Elliott and I had to take the bus home for the rest of the year. I put the crutches in one hand and hopped on one foot up the steps and took a seat near the front. Eric got on next, and as I could have guessed, he went and sat in the back. I shut my eyes and tried to fall asleep to block out the events from the day.

The bus dropped Eric and me off at our stop two blocks from our house, and we stood in silence, waiting for Kyle and Elliott. Well, Eric stood. I just sat down and let my crutches disappear into the snow.

When the elementary school bus finally pulled up, I could hear some commotion coming from inside, and it droned out the thin layer of ice that cracked under the bus as it came to a stop. Shadows of kids in winter jackets filled the windows, and a mocking laughter bellowed out of the bus when the driver opened the door. Elliott and Kyle came walking out quietly, both with their winter jacket hoods over their heads. This was not normal.

Eric must have felt the same uneasiness as I did, and he ran up to Kyle to see what was wrong. Kyle was crying and could barely get any words out. Elliott stood in the same spot and tightened his hood like he was trying to block out the rest of the world.

I approached Elliott and was greeted by a foul odor that lingered under my nose for a good ten seconds. Holding my breath to escape the nasty smell, I weaved my fingers into the small hole of Elliott's hood and opened it.

Mom used to say that eyes could tell a whole story if you looked hard enough. I'd never understood what that meant until I saw Elliott that day. His eyes were swollen with tears, and I could feel—like, *actually* feel—the exhaustion in his body. Whatever had happened to Elliott, it wasn't good.

"I need a tissue," Elliott said, his eyes still fixed on me.

That was obvious. He had a flowing waterfall of boogers hanging out of his nose.

"I don't have a tissue," I said and stepped back. "What in the world happened?"

"Zach Strouder," Eric quickly interrupted. "That's what happened."

Zach Strouder. It is one of those names that always makes you appreciate being out of elementary school. Zach is a three-time third grader, meaning he's repeated the third grade not just once or twice but three times. Even Grace didn't mess with Zach when we were in his class three years ago. He was a bully then, so by now he was a *professional* bully. He could get kids to do anything, and I mean *anything*.

"What did he do, Elliott? Did he mess with you?" I asked. I could feel my brotherly defensive instincts kick in.

"Ummm . . ." Elliott hesitated. "He . . . he made me pee my pants."

"How can someone *make* someone else pee their pants?"

"You don't know, Matt! He's mean! You have no idea!" Elliott sobbed. Kyle joined in, and they cried together in their separate spots.

Eric took control of the situation. "All right, let's walk home and get you both cleaned up. Then we'll tell our parents when we get home, okay?"

We herded Elliott and Kyle down the sidewalk, and they sniffled all the way home. When it came time to split to our own houses, Eric grabbed my crutch and pulled me close.

"Meet me at 10:00 tonight in the street," he whispered.

"Why? It's a school night," I asked.

"Because tonight, Zach Strouder is going to get it, and you're gonna help me."

Eric let go of me and walked inside with his brother. The fact that Eric had talked to me was shocking enough, but our mission shocked me even more. Whatever Eric had planned, Zach Strouder was in for a load of trouble.

CHAPTER 25
ZACH STROUDER'S CURVEBALL

I went to bed shortly after Elliott told Mom and Dad what happened. Dad blew his top, and Mom was so distraught that she tried calling the principal at 8:00 at night. No one answered.

I lay in bed till 10:00, then crept outside. It was easier than you think. Dad was snoring on the living room couch, and Mom was passed out in her room. I only had to put on my snow pants and jacket and walk out the front door. It was that simple, but that doesn't mean it wasn't risky. I could get grounded for the rest of my life, but for Elliott and Kyle, it was worth it.

The ground was still masked with snow, which made navigating it on crutches almost impossible. Luckily, Eric must have thought about it, and I found him sitting under the streetlamp with a rope and sled.

"Hop in," he said. "We have to make this a quick trip."

"Where are we going?" I asked, throwing my crutches into the plastic sled.

Eric grabbed the rope. "Zach's house."

"What? Are you serious?! No way, Eric. Let's talk about this first."

"There's nothing to talk about! Get in the sled." Eric pointed at the cracked plastic sled.

So we just go from not talking at all to making a plan to get revenge and possibly get in super *big* trouble? Didn't he want to talk about Grace? The soccer game? Our friendship?! I didn't understand why Eric wanted my help after ignoring me for the past month. So I asked.

"Why do you even need my help, Eric? Can't you do it yourself?"

Eric looked out into the black street. "I'm tired of Zach always getting away with everything. The kid is a jerk. Look, do you want to help or not?"

I wanted to help. I wanted Zach to be sorry. But what I wanted more was my friendship with Eric back. I had no idea what we were about to do, but I did know one thing: I missed Eric. I had to go.

I swung my feet into the sled and set my crutches down. "Wait. Isn't Zach's house, like, two miles from here?" I asked.

"You're right. Better get moving," he said and started jogging faster.

My head whipped back and smacked the sled, but I held tight to my only mode of transportation. If I let go now, it would be impossible to walk home in the snow with crutches.

Eric and I were like a dogsled team. I was the driver, and he was the dog, but it was a team effort for the next half hour. Eric kept his head down to focus, and I gave the directions.

"Left, Eric! No! More to the left!" I yelled.

He shifted at my command, and we cruised block after block. I really wanted to yell, "Mush!" but I think that would have ruined our groove.

After thirty minutes of mushing and running, Eric came to a halt and let the sled slowly glide across the snow. We had reached the outskirts of our neighborhood, and I could barely see Zach's house across the cow field.

Eric caught his breath and grabbed the rope of the sled again. "Don't make a sound, Matt. We need to walk past the sleeping cows. If they wake up, we're toast."

I still didn't know what we were going to do at Zach's house, but at this point I was at the mercy of Eric's plan. I was too far away from home to try to walk, and I needed him to get back.

Eric moved the barbed-wired fence and pulled me through without a scratch. The field was darker than the street, and the eerie outline of sleeping cows was the only thing separating us from Zach's house.

If that wasn't bad enough, the foul stench of cow manure was unbearable; I covered my mouth to stop from throwing up.

Eric's steps were small and stealthy but still echoed in the night. I shut my eyes and prayed we wouldn't get trampled by cows. It was terrifying being in the unknown.

Suddenly, the noise of Eric's crunchy footsteps stopped, and the sled slowly slid into the back of his ankles.

"Don't. Move," Eric whispered.

I squinted my eyes to get a look. Blocking the stars from shining was the shadow of a large bull. I could hear its heavy, machinelike breathing, and we were so close the warmth from the bull's breath grazed my cheeks.

Eric leaned back and pushed the sled. Each time his foot stepped in the snow, I waited for the bull to spring awake and trample us. I closed my eyes again and held tight to my crutches.

After a few minutes, Eric's footsteps finally stopped, and I opened my eyes.

"We're here," Eric whispered. He grabbed my hand to help me up. "Can you walk?"

"Yeah, I'll manage. What are we going to do?" My brain had tried to solve this question the entire trip, but I still had no idea what Eric wanted to do.

"Follow me," he said.

I grabbed my crutches, and we followed the outline of Zach's brick house until we came to a window. It was then that Eric laid out his plan.

"This is Zach's room, and we're gonna flood it."

"We're gonna what?!" I shouted.

"Shhhh!" Eric slapped my arm. "You wanna get caught? We going to crack his window open, shove that garden hose in there, and turn it on. When he wakes up, his room will be a winter wonderland of ice and snow." His lips curled, and he laughed under his breath. "Sound good to you?"

I wish all choices in life were easy. The plan did sound good, but it also didn't. I wanted Zach to pay for what he did to our brothers, but I also didn't want anyone else to get hurt. Jenna got hurt. I *was* hurt. But getting soaked with icy-cold water shouldn't hurt Zach, right? Maybe just teach him a lesson?

I finally nodded my head. "I hope this plan doesn't backfire," I said.

Eric went around the corner, and I heard the squeaking

sound of rusted metal. He returned with the hose already running with cold water. I grabbed the window frame and gave it a nudge up, just enough space for Eric to slide the hose in. The water splashed onto the floor and made its way around the carpeted room.

As the water soaked into every inch of Zach's room, a muffled voice rose from Zach's bed. "Mmmmm. Mommy, is that you?"

Eric ducked, but I kept my head in the window. The sheets ruffled in the bed, and Zach turned over. His smug face lifted off the pillow, and I watched as he sat up in bed, rubbing his eyes.

Our prank was about to be ruined, so I made a change in Eric's plan he didn't expect—I reeled in the hose and pressed my thumb against the flowing water, turning it into a spraying water cannon.

"Take that!" I yelled and aimed the shooting water directly at Zach.

Even in the dim light, I was able to see the water hit him directly in the face. It knocked him to his side, and he fell out of bed.

"Ahhhhhh!" Zach screamed. He was tangled in the sheets, making him defenseless as the cold water soaked him from head to toe. "Stop it! STOP IT!"

"That's for Kyle and Elliott!" Eric yelled back. "Serves you right!"

Zach made an attempt to run out of his room, but he ran right into his own door and fell—*smack*—to the floor. "Mom! Mooooom! Hurry! Someone's here!"

I shot one last blast of water and dropped the hose.

"Let's get outta here!" I yelled and dived into the sled with my crutches.

Eric grabbed the rope and sprinted into the field. The cows awoke from their sleep and scattered like mice from a cat. I could feel the pounding of their hooves, and the sled shook violently. Snow and cow patties flew in all directions as the cows panicked. It was an out-of-control stampede! I shut my eyes again and prayed we wouldn't be crushed flat.

"Duck!" Eric yelled.

I put my crutches between my legs just as the barbed-wire fence caught the tip of my hood. The sled glided straight into the curb of the sidewalk and shot me out into a snowbank.

I sat up to make sure I was still alive and gathered my crutches from the small hill. Eric met me under the street-light, which showed his neck covered in snow-dusted cow dung.

"Haha! Gross! Look at your face!" I laughed.

"Ah, sick! Get it off me!" Eric yelled and brushed the poop off his neck. "That's nasty!"

We sat and laughed in the snow till our bellies hurt. "Oh man, that was incredible! I can't believe we did that!" I said.

"I know, right? That was awesome!" Eric grabbed the rope and began the long walk home. We had escaped the cow field—barely. We talked all the way back, but not just about soaking Zach with freezing-cold water. We talked about school, soccer, Eric's new friends, and even Grace.

"Hey, I'm sorry that I've been mean lately. I'm over the Grace thing now. It was immature," Eric admitted. "I don't know why it took me so long to get over it."

"No worries," I said. "I'm just glad to hang out with you again." And just like that, our friendship was back on track.

"So how is, you know, the Curse?" Eric asked.

I could tell he was curious, especially since we hadn't talked in months.

"It hasn't stopped, if that's what you mean," I said. I didn't know what else to tell him. The Curse was becoming so normal now that it was hard to think of a life without it.

"Well, we'll figure it out. All right?" he encouraged.

I nodded.

When we got home, I sneaked back inside the house just as easily as I had sneaked out. Before I went to bed, though, I opened the door to Elliott's room and knelt down to whisper in his ear.

"We got Zach Strouder for you, Elliott. He won't bother you anymore."

Elliott rolled over and smiled with his eyes still shut. "Mmmm. Thanks," he mumbled and dozed back off to sleep town.

My brotherly duty was fulfilled. I'd gotten revenge for Elliott, and it felt good. But you know what felt better? Having my best friend back. Maybe next time we could simply *talk* about our problems, though, you know? That sounds easier than getting in a fight during a soccer game or running through a field of cow poop together.

Or maybe it isn't. Friendships are tricky.

I lay in bed and replayed the prank in my head until I realized something else: life wasn't the only thing that could throw curveballs—*I* could too. And I'd just given one to Zach Strouder.

CHAPTER 26
TOE EIGHT

Zach Strouder didn't pick on Elliott or Kyle the rest of the week or the week after. He must have put the pieces together and figured out that if he messed with them again, he would get more than just ice-cold water in his face in the middle of the night.

I didn't expect Elliott to talk to me about the event anymore, but he did. His timing wasn't the best, though.

"Hey, can you see me?!" Elliott said as he stuck a few of his fingers beneath the bathroom door. "I have something for you!"

"I'm on the toilet, Elliott," I muttered. "Can't it wait till I'm done?"

Suddenly, a piece of folded paper shot underneath the door and landed right between my feet. I opened it up, and there was a note scribbled on it.

Thank you for getting Sach.

I smiled and looked at the door. I could see a shadow, which meant Elliott hadn't left.

"You're welcome," I said, while staring at the note. "Next time someone wants to pick on you, though, just stand up to them like you do with me. No one will mess with you then!"

Elliott laughed, and then I heard his feet patter down the hallway. Hopefully, he would take my advice, because sometimes a little confidence in yourself is all it takes to scare a bully away.

The trip to Zach's house had done more than just scare Zach too. It had patched the friendship between Eric and me. We started doing everything together again and even spent time practicing karate moves in my room. Actually, I just watched, because my toes were still throbbing from being pulled on a sled through cow dung at high speeds.

Or maybe it was the soccer playing. Yeah, my actions were definitely catching up to me. Any pressure on either of my feet hurt, and I couldn't cover it up. The crutches weren't helping, and Dad noticed over the weekend.

"I'm taking you back to urgent care," Dad said.

There was no use arguing, so I walked on my heels to the garage and pulled myself up into the seat. Urgent care. Again. For the third time. I felt like my life was a movie being rewound and played again. The only difference was that this time I hadn't broken any *new* toes.

The receptionist greeted us with an enthusiastic smile and clap. "Good afternoon! What can I help you with?"

"I called a few minutes ago. The last name is Sprouts," informed Dad.

"Oh yes, please come with me." The receptionist patted me on the shoulder and led us to a small room in the back of the hallway. "Wait here for the doctor, okay, buddy?" She patted me again and left.

"What's her deal? I asked Dad.

"Hey, watch your tone." Dad flipped through a small pamphlet. "She was trying to be friendly."

The doctor walked in while Dad was reading.

"Well, well! Nice to see you both again!" she said. "What seems to be the trouble today?"

Dad put down the pamphlet and got straight to the point. "Matt broke a few more toes, and I don't think they're healing. We were hoping you could take a look?"

"Certainly, certainly. We'll make sure that everything is setting correctly and that the bones are doing what they need to do. Matt, will you do me a favor? Can you kick off your shoes and lie down on that table? Make sure not to kick that machine on your way in or you'll owe us a few million dollars haha!"

"That's fine. My brother could pay you. He's going to be a bazillion-trillionaire someday," I said as I slid my feet into the machine.

"What?" The doctor looked at Dad for an answer.

"Never mind," I said. "I was being sarcastic."

"Oh." The doctor continued to fiddle with some buttons. "Anyway, relax your head and lean back. This will take a few minutes," she warned. She adjusted some switches on the giant tube and ordered that I remain still. Dad stepped into a back room before the machine launched into a series of humming and buzzing noises that made it seem like the tube was going to blast off into space. After a few minutes, it was all over.

"All righty. Let's see what you got. Have a seat over here," the doctor continued.

Dad came back in, picked me up, and moved me to a chair on the far side of the room next to a computer screen mounted on the wall. The doctor kept talking while she pulled up some pictures.

"All right, see that?" she pointed to some bones on the screen. "That's your right foot, Matt. And those are your broken toes there." She took out a red marker and circled three toes. "The only ones not broken are the pinky toe and one next to it."

The doctor had made a mistake. "I only broke *two* toes," I announced. "I didn't break the middle one."

"No. You definitely broke three," she said and tapped the screen again.

I was getting frustrated. She obviously wasn't listening to me. "I just told you: I only broke *two* snowboarding. The ski medic in Telluride told me."

"He's telling the truth," Dad added. "Dylan said he only broke two."

The doctor looked at us and laughed. "Well, I guess Dylan was wrong, then, wasn't he? These X-rays don't lie. Do you see the cracks in that toe there? And there? And there? All three are broken. I don't know what else to tell you."

I stared at the X-ray in disbelief. How could I not know I'd broken another toe?

"Have you been on crutches or in a wheelchair before? Matt? Matt?"

I was still in shock, and the noises around me bounced off my head. The Curse had fooled me. Without me even knowing, it had broken another toe.

Dad's voiced boomed and broke my concentration. "Matt. The doctor asked you a question."

"Sorry," I said. "I've been on crutches for a few weeks."

"No, no, no." The doctor shook her head. "That won't

do. I'm going to get you a wheelchair. You shouldn't be putting any pressure at all on *either* foot for at least another two weeks. Maybe more."

"Please!" I yelled. "I'll just crawl, okay? I don't need anything else. Dad!"

"Be serious, Matt," Dad grabbed my arm to calm me down. "If you don't do what the doctor says, you could damage your foot further."

Helpless. That's about all I felt right then. But that's not all. *The feeling* was there. It didn't sneak up on me this time and catch me off guard. I had expected it to show up at some point, but I didn't think I would react how I did.

"GO AWAY!" I yelled. "LEAVE ME ALONE!"

The doctor and Dad jumped back, and I kept screaming.

"You think you can win? You think you can beat me?! I will defeat you! I will!"

Dad grabbed me by the shoulders and stuck his face right in front of mine. "Whoa! Whoa, Matt! It's okay! What is going on?"

And then I lost it. I cried harder than I have ever cried in my entire life.

The doctor left the room. I sat there with Dad, and he just held me while *the feeling* slowly disappeared.

"It's okay, buddy. It's okay. Let's finish this up and get you home, okay?"

I nodded, and the doctor appeared back in the room. She showed us to a freezing-cold waiting room filled with other miserable-looking people and told us to wait for a few minutes. I was frowning so hard my forehead hurt, and I shoved my hands in my pockets to keep warm. I could feel Dad looking at me, but I didn't look back. Staring at the floor was a better option. I felt humiliated.

"I'm going to fill out the rest of the paperwork," Dad said. "Don't go crawling off, okay?"

"Haha," I muttered. I kept my focus on the floor. There was a tiny ant scuttling back and forth between the cracks of the tile. He seemed happy. He hadn't broken any toes. He just kept on walking like it wasn't a big deal. He was free to do whatever he wanted. Is that how the Curse sees me? Like some walking ant waiting to be crushed? I wondered what that power felt like. I raised my foot to squash him, to feel that same power, but I couldn't do it. I might be the Cursed Kid, but I was not the Curse. I was better than that.

Just then, some old lady walked into the waiting room. She sat down right next to me and tapped my arm with her bony finger.

"Well, hello, Mr. Sprouts. Enjoying your time viewing ants, I see."

My body stiffened while my head turned to see my new neighbor. It was Mrs. Klinkle.

"I . . . um . . . I just . . ." was all I could out. I glanced back at the front desk to see whether Dad could save me, but he was still filling out forms.

Mrs. Klinkle put her bony hand on my shoulder and squeezed her nails into my skin.

"Now, what on earth are you doing here again? Break another toe?!" Mrs. Klinkle crackled and slapped her knee. "Oh, wouldn't that be some irony? You breaking another toe. Ha!"

I had no idea what she wanted from me. What was she doing at the urgent care anyway? Had the Curse sent her to torture me some more?

She cackled one last time and then looked me straight in the eye. "I asked you a question, Mr. Sprouts. Don't be rude to your elders. Why are you here?"

"I, um, broke another toe."

Mrs. Klinkle covered her mouth like she was about to throw up. Her cheeks puffed, and her face turned red until whatever she was trying to stop came out.

"Bwaahaha! That is the funniest thing I have heard all

day! Have many toes have you broken? Twenty?! What an unlucky little boy!" She let her head fall backward, and the laughter echoed throughout the room.

Dad looked at me and shook his head, going back to his papers.

"Beat it, Mrs. Klinkle. Just let me sit here."

"Well, if you're not going to talk to me, then I'll just talk to you. I heard you have the Curse."

I kept my mouth shut.

"And I've heard that the Curse has been causing you some problems—problems with your toes. Is that right?"

I didn't know how she knew, but I stayed quiet.

"What if"—her tone lifted—"I said I could help you?"

Help? Mrs. Klinkle? Yeah, right. And maybe next I would win the lottery or fly to the moon. Still, she at least had my attention.

I mustered up a grunt. "What did you say?"

"Don't act like you didn't hear me, Sprouts. Do you want my help or not?"

I turned around to look the old grape lady in the face. It was a stare-down, and I didn't break eye contact.

"How do I know you're not just messin' with me?" I said. "How do I know you're not just trying to make me feel even worse?"

"You're out of time to wonder about those questions, aren't you? Don't you want to be free of the Curse? This is your last chance."

The double doors to the doctor's office flew open, and they spit out a wheelchair. I expected to see a regular-looking wheelchair. But it wasn't. The previous owner had put stickers on it—and not just any stickers; they were cute baby pandas wearing diapers. It was not my style, not at all.

Before the wheelchair made it all the way to me, one of the wheels jammed. The doctor muttered something, gave one of the wheels a swift kick, and then parked it by the office wall.

I looked back at Mrs. Klinkle, then back at the oddly decorated wheelchair. It was either take Mrs. Klinkle's help or continue getting hurt. The choice was obvious, so I had to take it.

I turned to Mrs. Klinkle, who was trying hard not to laugh at the stickers. "I'll take your help," I said. "Anything to get the Curse away from me."

Mrs. Klinkle nodded and took out a small piece of crumpled paper from her pocket. She slowly stood up, took my hand in hers, and folded the paper into my palm. "You may think you are all alone. Mr. Sprouts, the Cursed Kid. Hmph!" she smirked. "Did you ever stop to think maybe, just maybe, someone as old as me might know a thing or two about curses? Why do you think I had you read that passage in class? You think that was just a coincidence?"

"I, uh . . ." was all I could get out.

"The world is not so small, Mr. Sprouts. You need to remember that. Over the years, some of us have learned secrets. And lucky for you, I happen to have one to share with you."

"What's this?" I asked, staring at the paper ball.

Mrs. Klinkle turned and started to walk toward the double doors to the doctor's office.

"Hey! Where are you going? What is this? You can't just give me a sheet of paper and walk away!"

The old grape lady didn't even acknowledge my voice. She pushed the double doors open and disappeared.

I shook my fist toward the door. "All you did was give me a dirty piece of paper!"

Dad came over and grabbed my wrists. "Stop it, Matt! You're embarrassing yourself."

"No, Dad, *that's* embarrassing!" I pointed at the stickers, which I realized were glittery as the light came in from the window.

Dad shook his head, picked me up, and put me in the wheelchair, next to my new diaper-wearing-panda neighbors. He wheeled me out the door, and I opened the sheet of paper to tear it into a million pieces. But I stopped. Four words, written in purple pen, were in the center of the page:

"Go visit Ben Hoodland."

I never did find out why Mrs. Klinkle was at the urgent care. But that note proved to be super helpful anyway—that's for sure.

CHAPTER 27
THE LEGEND OF BREAKABLE BEN

Ben Hoodland. No one *ever* said that kid's last name out loud. If you didn't know him, you'd think his name was boring enough—so boring you'd forget it the next day if someone asked you. If you went to Centennial Middle School, though, you knew who Ben was. You had to know. It was impossible not to know. Everyone knew the stories, and everyone knew his true name: Breakable Ben.

They say he was the unluckiest kid in the middle school. Some say he broke every bus in the district. Others say he once broke the aquarium in the science room—twice! I even heard one kid say Breakable Ben had set the school on fire. They were all rumors, though, because no one really knew *why* he had been kicked out of school. To us, the stories were just a legend.

"That's who you're supposed to see?" Grace gasped. "No one has ever been to his house before. Do you even know where it is? How are you going to talk to him? How will you . . ."

I'd called Grace to explain the situation. That was a mistake. I couldn't even get one word in as she pummeled me with questions.

"How should we get you there? Can I push you? What if the Curse strikes again? Then what?"

"Look, Grace," I said. "I don't expect you to help. I just thought I would tell you what had happened."

"Oh. Well, I *want* to help. I'll be over in a little bit, and we can go visit Ben together—I mean Breakable Ben—even if I do have to push you all the way there."

I clicked the phone off and let it fall to my lap. It was clear the Curse was winning and I was running out of options. The note from Mrs. Klinkle was my last chance to change things, so I had to try. Even if the help *was* coming from Mrs. Klinkle.

While I waited for Grace, Gummers took a liking to my chair. He hopped on my lap and purred while I watched Elliott and Kyle come into the kitchen.

"Whatcha doing, Matt?" Kyle said. He was gnawing on a giant cookie.

Elliott laughed and joined in.

"Oh, wait. You're doing nothing 'cuz your toes are broke! Ha!" He and Kyle danced in a circle with their fingers pointed toward the sky like they'd just said the best, most humorous joke in the world.

I let them dance. They looked silly doing it, anyway.

They continued to make jokes about the Curse while I waited for Grace to show up. Gummers kept me company, and I plotted what I would say to Breakable Ben. I only knew him as a rumor—someone who *might* have existed. How was he going to be able to help? Was he magic? Did he have a potion to drop on me? A chant? If any of the rumors about him were true, he was probably going to be the only one who might have some new information about the Curse.

The gravel crunched in the driveway, and Grace's parents' gray minivan appeared. Grace spotted me in the window and waved from the passenger seat. I could see more bodies in the van, though, and Grace didn't have any siblings. As soon as the van stopped, Henry and John jumped out from the back seats, and Grace led them to the front door.

"Hey, guys. What are you doing here?" I said, out of breath. Rolling myself in the rusty wheelchair to the front door had been hard work.

Henry and John looked at Grace. "Um . . . we wanted to come?" they said in unison.

"That's right!" Grace smiled. "They want to be there when you meet Ben. We're your support team!"

It was obvious that Grace had forced them to come. Henry and John both looked nervous and would have never volunteered to meet someone as notorious as Breakable Ben.

"Looks like the whole gang is here," a familiar voice said. Eric emerged from the corner of the hallway, tossing a football up and down. Before I could even ask, Grace answered my question.

"I called Eric and asked if he could come too!" I could tell she was proud of herself, and her excitement beamed from her cheeks.

"I'm sick of you breaking your toes. Time we solve this Curse thing for real," Eric said, tossing me the football.

Gummers ran for cover.

"Thanks, guys. But, really, I think I can do it myself." I was trying to sound convincing, but it came off weak.

"Whatever, Sprouts!" Eric was in my face, but he was smiling. "We're coming with you. You don't have a choice anyway. You going to stop us from your chair?"

That was the end of the conversation. Eric took a tight grip on the wheelchair and pushed me out the front door, with Grace, Henry, and John behind us. There was no turning back now, but I didn't really have a choice in that.

"Hey, Grace, do you even know how to get there?" I said. All this talk of Breakable Ben, and I didn't even know where the guy lived.

"Uh-huh. I forced—I mean *asked*—some kids from school where I could find him. He actually lives just a mile from here," she smiled.

Who would have thought? The legend, Breakable Ben, actually lived close to me, Matt Sprouts—the Cursed Kid. I couldn't wait to meet this guy. I could sense something big was going to happen.

It was cold out, but luckily there wasn't much snow on the street anymore. Besides the trees on either side of the road, Grace, Eric, John, Henry, and I were the only living things around. The streets were quiet. The houses along the road seemed empty. The only noise that filled the space was the squeaking from my wheelchair. It would have annoyed me, but I was distracted by Grace. She walked alongside me, holding my hand as Eric pushed me down the street.

We rounded Edgar Street onto Leather Ridge, and Grace stopped us to point out the house. "That's gotta be it."

We all found ourselves staring at a green house. The shingles were chipped, the sidewalk was bent, and the windows were foggy. It looked like multiple people had tried to clean it multiple times, but each time was unlucky and slipped and fell and stopped halfway. Maybe that was the power of the Curse. Once it got so bad, it got other people in too.

"Do we knock on the door or wait for it to blow over

in the wind?" Eric said. He walked to the battered gate that separated the road from the house. "Seriously, this place is a dump."

"I'm fine with waiting," Henry said. He turned around and looked back down the road. "Or we could just go."

"Yeah, that sounds good. I doubt anyone lives here anyway," John agreed and wiped the fog from his glasses.

"Are you all serious?" Grace's hand tightened so hard around mine that it hurt. "If none of you babies will go to the door, then I'll do it!"

Before anyone could stop her, Grace opened the fence and walked straight up to the door. She didn't even bother to knock.

"Hello? We're here to see Ben! Is he home? Ben? Are you in there?" she screamed.

"Grace, calm down. We don't want to scare the guy," I said. "Just give it a minute."

"He's in there," she muttered. "I can sense it! Ben! Get out here and talk to us right now!"

If I were Ben, I would have gone to my room and locked the door. Grace was determined, and her bossy side was definitely showing. There was no stopping her.

But before Grace could scream out another demand, the door opened. There stood a boy, no taller than Grace. His shaggy blond hair covered his face, but his outfit was more distracting. He was only wearing blue jean overalls that were three sizes too large.

"Well, aren't you going to invite us in?" Grace asked, tapping her foot on the frame of the door. The boy walked inside, and Grace followed into the darkness.

"Did she just go in with that kid?" Henry asked.

"Yeah, she did," Eric laughed. "Come on, guys. Let's go."

Eric, Henry, and John pushed me across the snowy lawn and into the entrance of Ben's house. Grace was sitting on the floor, poking a small box turtle on its shell—it seemed unamused by her gesture. The boy was sitting in a rocking chair, but it was too big for him. The armrests were above his shoulders.

"Are you Ben?" I asked. I had pictured Breakable Ben to be much larger, not the small, scruffy kid in overalls who sat before us. So I'd had to ask.

"Yeah. Who wants to know?" Ben answered.

"Um, I do. I was told you could help me." It was strange asking such a small person for help.

"Why should I?" he asked. He leaned forward in his chair to look at me.

"Because he's cursed!" John blurted out. Everyone looked at John, including the turtle. John covered his mouth like he'd caused an accident. "Um, sorry. I didn't mean to yell."

"Who's cursed?" Ben asked. "Is it you?" He pointed at my chest and stared deeply into my eyes. Even from a small person, it was intimidating.

"Yeah, it's me," I sulked. I looked down at the floor. "I've run out of options. My toes keep breaking, all because of something I did last summer. I think I'm cursed. Sounds silly, doesn't it?"

Ben got up from his big chair and studied me. He ran his small hands down my feet until he got to my toes. He poked each one, maybe to test whether they were alive or something.

"And what do you expect me to do about it?" he asked.

"We were hoping you could stop the Curse," Grace said.

"Ha! I can't stop it," Ben giggled. He stood up and poked me in the chest. "Only *you* can."

"And how do you know that?" I asked.

"Because I was just like you. Cursed. But I figured it out." Ben turned his back to us and stared at his chair.

"Then why do they call you 'Breakable Ben'?"

"Do I really have to explain it? Don't you know the stories?" he said, shocked.

All of us looked around like we had no idea what he was talking about. But we did. We all knew the stories. We stayed quiet, though, and I hoped to hear the truth.

Ben sat back down in his oversized chair and let out a sigh. "Uh, fine. I'll tell." He straightened the straps on his overalls and leaned his head back in the chair. "Two years ago, I broke a vase. Not just any vase—I broke the giant Swan Vase from the museum in town."

"That was you?!" Henry interrupted. "Our teacher told us that it fell over because it was old! How did you break it?"

"If you shut your mouth, maybe you'll find out," Ben

snapped. "Anyway, I was trying to climb it to see what was in there. When you went there on field trips, didn't you want to know? It was so huge; I knew something had to be in it. When our tour guide took the class to the next room, I stayed behind and started climbin'. It was easy. I got to the top in, like, ten—no, *five*—seconds."

He held his hand up so we could all count his fingers.

"But when I got to the top and tried to sit down, the vase wobbled, and I couldn't find my balance. I jumped, and the vase shattered."

"Did you get caught?!" Henry interrupted again.

"No one caught me that day, but the Curse did," Ben said and pointed right at me. "For the next few weeks, anything I touched broke. The school bus I rode broke down. I busted the aquarium in science class. My mom pulled me out so I wouldn't destroy the school, but at home it got worse. I broke the TV remote. The TV. My computer. My pencils. The shower. The toilet . . ."

"Is that why your house is so nasty?" Henry asked.

Grace glared at Henry, while the turtle put its head in its shell. The tension was thick.

Ben moved like he was going to hit Henry but sat back down. "Yeah, that's why. By the time I figured out how to break the Curse, I'd broken almost everything." He looked around the room like he was searching for something. "It's too bad. I used to have some nice stuff."

My mind was racing. What if I didn't figure out how to break the Curse? Would I break every bone in my body? I needed an answer.

"How did you do it?" I asked slowly. "How did you break the Curse?"

Ben took out a ball of duct tape from his pocket and tossed it in the air to himself. "Eventually, I fessed up and told my parents—you know, about the Swan Vase. But that didn't stop the Curse. Not yet. I had to *fix* the vase. The museum had kept all the pieces from the vase and had been working on putting it back together all year. My parents made me go to the museum and help every day for the rest of sixth grade until it was done. So I guess the only way to break the Curse is to fix what you broke. That's my theory."

"That might be hard to do for Matt, though." Eric was leaning against the door with his arms folded. "He broke my sister's collarbone, and it healed already."

Everyone was staring at me. My eyes wiggled back and forth while my brain tried to find a hole in Ben's statement. If the solution to stopping the Curse was to fix what I had broken, then I would be cursed forever. Jenna's collarbone had healed by the time summer vacation was over. How in the world could I go back and fix it? It was impossible.

"What's wrong? Cat got your tongue?" Ben asked.

"I don't think I can do it. I've lost. I don't think I can win," I muttered.

Grace patted me on the back, and Eric let out a long, disappointed sigh. Henry and John just did what they did best and stared at the floor. We all felt defeated.

Ben stood up and looked at an invisible watch on his wrist. "No use in you taking up space in my living room, then. Time's up. I don't want any chance of the Curse coming back to me. No way, no how. You guys all scram."

"Oh wow, you're a nice guy. Can't you see Matt is upset? What is he supposed to do?" Grace challenged. "There must be another way to stop it!"

"Then I guess he'll have to figure it out on his own. Get out of here. All of you! Now!" Ben yelled and kicked the dust from the floor in our faces. Eric spit in Ben's direction, then I wheeled out the door. Henry, Grace, Eric, and John ran out behind me, and we all found ourselves staring at the broken greenhouse, with its broken fence and shattered windows. Our time with the legendary Breakable Ben was officially over.

Eric couldn't believe it either. "No wonder he doesn't go to school anymore and has to be homeschooled."

"Shhh!" Grace tried to whisper, but I could hear it all.

"Eric! Matt doesn't need to hear that right now. He's obviously having a hard time with this."

"He might as well," John added. "He's going to have to deal with it for the rest of his life . . ."

"John! Stop it. Matt is going to hear!"

"It doesn't matter, Grace," Henry continued. "It's over. Maybe we can just get Matt a really cool plastic bubble to walk in for the rest of his life."

While the four of them argued over whether I was going to be cursed for the rest of my life, I stood up.

"And all he needs is just a little—Matt?!" Grace turned and put both her hands on my shoulders. "You need to sit down. You can't walk! You need rest."

Something snapped in my brain. I don't know what it was—maybe it happened because I was so frustrated. Maybe it happened because I was sick of being looked after like a pet dog. Or maybe it was the Curse and cold, dark nothingness setting another broken toe into motion. Whatever it was, it made me run. Or at least *try* to run.

"Matt, what are you doing?!" Grace yelled, but it was too late.

I stood on the sides of my feet to avoid the pain in my toes and ran fast as I could. My legs were locked tight, and I wasn't moving much faster than Breakable Ben's turtle. It didn't matter, though. For those first few steps, I was free. My mind blocked out the Curse and all the broken-toe memories. I could have run forever that day.

But I didn't get far—not far at all. The curb of the sidewalk caught me, and I smashed my right foot into it and went face-first into the snow. Before I could wipe the snow off my face, Grace, Henry, John, and Eric grabbed my jacket and lifted me into the wheelchair.

"What were you thinking?! Are you trying to get yourself hurt?" Grace yelled and brushed the snow from the top of my head. She kept blabbering something about using my common sense, but I was looking at my right foot.

The pain was familiar, but I could tolerate it. I didn't bother to remove my shoe or sock. Any kid could have guessed what was under there. The Curse had struck again and claimed toes nine and ten.

Eric squatted down in front of the wheelchair to look me in the face, but I didn't return the gesture.

"Are you okay?" he said, concern in his voice. "You freaked us all out."

I didn't need to tell him about the broken toes. It didn't hurt that bad.

"Yeah. I'm fine. Let's go home. I want to be alone."

And that's what we did. Not one of us spoke the rest of the walk home, not even Grace. What would we talk about anyways? It was clear the Curse had set us all up for another failure, and talking about it wouldn't change a thing. Silence was the best option.

When we got home, Eric pushed me all the way up to the front door. Before anyone else said anything, Grace asked Eric, Henry, and John to give us some time alone. They backed up, and Grace took my hand in hers, and we stared at my front door together.

"What are you going to tell your parents?" Grace asked, her voice genuine but filled with worry.

"I don't know what to tell them. I don't know whether they'll even believe me."

Grace stroked my hand with her thumb and sighed.

"I just don't get it, Grace," I continued. "I mean, all I did was break Jenna's collarbone. It was a complete accident, and I apologized for it! Why should I be cursed for that?"

"Yeah, but you ruined her summer too," Grace said, "and you told me she was miserable. Remember?"

I paused. "Wait. What did you say?"

"Um . . . I said you ruined her summer?" Grace responded hesitantly.

The gears in my head were turning faster than they ever had before.

"Say it again," I said.

She turned to make sure I wasn't getting mad at her. And I wasn't. I was the exact opposite.

"Okay . . ." she hesitated. "I said you ruined her summer. What's this about, Matt?" she asked.

I pulled Grace down close to me and smiled. "Grace. Go get Henry, John, and Eric. I just figured out how to break the Curse."

CHAPTER 28
JENNA'S SURPRISE

Some of the simplest ideas take time. Did you know it took over two hundred years for someone to invent the eraser? People used bread to erase their pencil marks, then one day some genius decided to use rubber. Why did it take so long to figure that out? It seems like an eight-year-old could have made that invention.

That's how I felt about my idea, like it had been right in front of me the whole time. It hadn't taken two hundred years to come up with, but the idea was brilliant. In fact, it was probably the best thing my brain had ever come up with. It took the rest of the weekend (after my parents took me to the doctor's for another checkup, of course), with help from Henry, Grace, John, and Eric to finish it, but by Sunday afternoon, everything was ready to go. The only thing my plan still needed was Jenna.

I shut the front door to our house and zipped up

my jacket so it covered my neck. It was freezing—fifteen degrees with wind. My boogers froze instantly, and my wheelchair turned into a metal icicle, but nothing could upset me that day. I smiled and rolled myself down the driveway to the Monklings' house. I was getting pretty talented in that wheelchair. I even popped a wheelie before I rang the doorbell.

As I hoped, Jenna answered. Even in her pajama pants and top, she was clearly excited to see me. Her two pigtails bounced as usual.

"Hey, Matt! Come in. It's cold out!" She grabbed the front wheels of my chair and tried to drag me in.

"Wait, wait!" I giggled. "Grab your jacket and come with me," I told her. "There's something I want to show you."

"But I have to stay—"

"It'll just take a second, Jenna. Come on," I begged.

It didn't take much longer to get her out of the house. She quickly put on her jacket and started pushing me down the sidewalk.

"What do you want to show me?" Jenna asked. She was excited and wouldn't stop asking questions.

"Just wait till we get to the door. Okay?" I laughed.

"What are all these cars doing at your house, Matt?"

"Just wait!"

Before we went into my house, I made Jenna close her eyes. It didn't really matter whether her eyes were shut, but it added a little more excitement to the whole thing.

I opened the door and made the final announcement. "All right, Jenna, open 'em!"

Jenna opened her eyes to my greatest creation ever. It had taken a lot of time and some money (with help from my parents), but it was *awesome*. I had turned my entire house, in the middle of the Colorado winter, into a summer party.

The walls were covered inch by inch in fake bright-yellow daisies. From the ceiling hung puffy white clouds made from giant cotton balls and feathery pillows. The ceiling fan was covered in a giant canvas cutout in the shape of the sun, and it spun as the lights flickered. The windows had their own display too. They were framed with party streamers, balloons, and cutouts of worldly places like the beaches of California and Costa Rica.

Jenna didn't say a word. She pushed me through the living room in awe. Her mouth hung open, and her eyes darted back and forth to absorb all the different colors that filled the house.

We got to the kitchen, and she stopped again. There were fancy glasses filled with pink lemonade around the counter and a giant watermelon split into small pieces by the stove. Hot dog buns were stacked as high as twenty by the sink, and a few pineapples bordered the shelves. In the dining room, small bowls of yellow and orange candies were placed in rows across the dining room table, and a tower of oranges and apples filled the center.

"Woooowww . . ." Jenna muttered and grabbed a slice of watermelon and shoveled it into her mouth.

"Well," I paused. "What do you think?"

"Shhh! I'm looking," she muttered. She continued into the family room.

Our giant television was paused on a still picture of a sunset, and the ground was covered in sleeping bags, pillows, and blankets. On the side table were three large salad bowls filled with popcorn, but that wasn't all. I leaned over in the chair and shut off the lights to the room. Greenish-yellow stars appeared on the ceiling and walls, and a large moon glowed from the top of the TV stand.

"How did you do all this?" she asked, wide eyed.

"We're not done yet," I laughed. "Let's go over to the garage door."

We went to the garage entry. Without having to ask, she opened the door to the biggest surprise of the day.

"SURPRISE!" yelled the crowd. Everyone appeared from behind the chairs and tables, just like we'd planned. It was everyone I could have thought to invite: Grace, Henry, John, Eric, Kyle, Kevin, Elliott, and even a few of Jenna's closest friends from school. I didn't know who they were, but Grace had taken care of contacting them.

"Oh my gosh! What is going on?!" Jenna screamed. "And how did you get that in here?!"

She was referring to the inflated pool in the middle of the garage. John's mom had brought it over and set it up the day before to make sure it would fit, and it had taken all night for the pool to fill with warm water. If that wasn't cool enough, Henry's dad had brought some all-weather carpet from his store and laid it next to the pool. It looked exactly like grass and covered the entire garage floor.

I poked Jenna on the shoulder to wake her up from the shock. "Well, what do you think?"

"What do I think? This is the most incredible thing I've ever seen in my entire life! The daisies, the watermelon, the stars . . . and the pool?! Why did you do all this?"

Her smile was bigger than I'd imagined it would be.

"I figured I owed you one. I mean, I *did* break your collarbone and threw your summer for a curveball. Right? So now you can enjoy the summer you didn't have," I grinned.

The least I could do was try to make it up to her. And this was the best way I knew how.

I had another reason for throwing the party too, though: a selfish one. Breakable Ben had mentioned that I had to fix whatever I'd broken in order to stop the Curse. I'd thought that was impossible, since Jenna's collarbone had already healed, but I'd been wrong. After Grace had mentioned that I'd wrecked Jenna's summer vacation, I'd known instantly what had truly been broken: I'd broken her *summer*. Since I wasn't able to fix Jenna's collarbone, I'd done the next best thing: I'd fixed her a nice summer vacation in the middle of winter.

The Curse might've been a Montrose legend, and maybe it was real, maybe it wasn't. In the end, I guess it doesn't really matter, because I owed it to Jenna to make things right. You can't just make a mistake and expect things to go back how they were without taking some action, you know? Plus, I don't want my friends to remember my mistakes. Or the broken collarbone. Or the broken toes.

I want them to remember I did the right thing.

"This isn't a magic fix-it," I told Jenna. "But I hope you know it's a start. And I do owe you a couple of games of hide-and-seek, I think."

Jenna smiled.

"More than a couple," she said.

It didn't take long for Grace and Jenna to meet either. She practically pushed me over to get to her.

"Hi, Jenna!" Grace beamed, while waving her hand in the air. "I'm Grace. Do you like it!?"

"This is all so cool!" Jenna said and then pointed toward the pool. "And where did you buy that from?!"

She was referring to the giant wooden letter *J* leaning up against the pool.

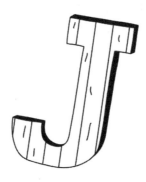

"Oh, I made that!" Grace said, slightly blushing.

"You did?!" Jenna said. "That's so cool!"

"It can even hang up in your room, Jenna! Here, let me show you the back!"

Jenna was super impressed as Grace explained how she made it, and the rest of the day was just as incredible. Jenna played in the pool with her friends and Grace; ate a summer BBQ dinner of hamburgers, hot dogs, and watermelon; and watched movies under the stars in the family room with all of us kids.

After the last movie ended, Jenna acame up to me and gave me a big hug.

"Thank you so much, Matt! I really needed this. It was *so* awesome. An awesome *start*," Jenna said.

It did feel like that. Like I was starting something. Being more aware of myself, maybe. Becoming more of a guy like my Dad.

I just smiled and let her enjoy the rest of the night with her friends. Grace leaned on my wheelchair, and we finished the movie holding hands under the light of the moon.

EPILOGUE
LEMONS
TO LEMONADE

Well, I'm happy to report that it's the end of sixth grade now, and I haven't broken a single bone since visiting Breakable Ben. Now my toes are healthy, and I can run faster than I did before. Maybe breaking the toes helped my legs get stronger. Who knows?

Best of all, I made some friends during that whole adventure. Henry and John started hanging out with me more often—and Eric too. He still had his seventh-grade gang of friends to hang out with, but we made time to bust karate moves on each other. Jenna would sit and watch most of the time, but I did catch her trying some karate kicks once.

Coach Reese became the new head coach of the soccer team, and no one was happier about that than I was.

Elliott never won his bazillion-trillion dollars, like the Magic 8 Ball said he would. I'll admit that I was hopeful it would come true.

Mrs. Klinkle stopped teaching later that year, which made life a lot easier. I heard she was happier retired anyway, and that made me happy. Even if I didn't like her, she still deserved a nice life. I tried visiting her at her house the day after Jenna's party, but she wouldn't answer the door.

Last but not least is Grace. I still tease her now and then about how bossy she can be, but she kind of likes it. Still, I couldn't be happier to have her by my side.

When life gives you lemons, you're supposed to make lemonade. But when life gives you ten broken toes, what do you do? I think it's different for everyone, but here's what I've learned through the Curse of ten broken toes. You can't let curveballs bother you. You have to tackle those problems and confront them head-on, whether you want to or not. And you set things right.

Maybe this advice will help if the Curse catches you.

Oh, and just one more thing. I *did* get into a little bit of trouble when summer started again. It wasn't my fault that Nora ate the sun, but I guess that's a story for another day . . .

ABOUT
THE AUTHOR

Matt Eicheldinger wasn't always a writer. He spent most of his childhood playing soccer, reading comics, and trying his best to stay out of trouble. Little did he know those moments would ultimately help craft the first book in his debut novel series, *Matt Sprouts and the Curse of the Ten Broken Toes*. Matt lives in Minnesota, with his wife and two children and tries to create new adventures with them whenever possible. When he's not writing, you can find him telling students stories in the classroom or trail running along the Minnesota River Bottoms.